STAY WITH ME

A BWWM RUSSIAN BILLIONAIRE ROMANCE

NOVEL

BY IMANI KING

Sign up for my newsletter to get the latest information, including updates on upcoming stories. Just enter this link into your browser address line:

http://eepurl.com/blwtg5

Check out more of my stories on amazon: http://www.amazon.com/author/imaniking

About **Stay With Me**

The show must go on. But a handsome Russian billionaire might be in the way…

Fashion designer Thania Walter's collection peaked in the fall/winter season. Now, Thania is the media's sweetheart, heading to an interview to talk about her upcoming designs. But it only takes one glimpse at a man on the set to make her crave him—dark, tall, and handsome, in an impeccable suit. Who could he be? She knows she shouldn't let him, but the delicious stranger invades Thania's mind.

Vladislav Sakharov is used to getting his way - be it with business contacts or women.

When he locks eyes with Thania, he knows he needs to have her in his arms. His billions have never been in the way of getting what he wants, yet Thania is fiercely independent, proud, and wary. But not even she can resist the Vlad's Russian charm...

Chapter 1

Thania

"I can't believe you're doing a photo shoot today! I'm so jealous," Daya said on the three-way call to her best friends, Asha and Thania.

"She deserves her success, Daya," Asha responded, but even through the phone, the sadness that seemed to follow her everywhere lately was apparent.

"I *know* she deserves it, especially after the incredible success of her clothing line," Daya said.

"Okay, girls," Thania interrupted. "No one is more surprised than me about how a simple magazine article could have such an impact on my career."

"A simple magazine article!" Disbelief laced Daya's tone. "You know as well as I do that *Modeliste* can make or break a designer's career. And a model's," she added, almost under her breath.

Thania knew that Daya hoped to someday model in the internationally-renowned fashion magazine, but so far she'd only had some modest success in their local metropolitan area.

"It'll happen for you, honey," Thania said softly into the phone, keenly aware that this newfound success of hers was changing the dynamic between the three best friends. "What work do you have coming up?" Thania asked, hoping to bring Daya to a happier place.

"Oh, I'm doing a runway show for Redmond's next week," Daya said, referring to a local high-end department store.

"That's great!" Thania said.

"When is it?" This came from Asha. "We want to come and see you in all of your model-strut glory," she added, and the three friends laughed.

Daya told them the details, and the women promised to make it to support their best friend.

"Don't you have to get going to the shoot, Thania?" asked Asha.

"Oh no, sweetheart. You're not getting off *that* easy. What's going on in your life?" Thania asked Asha, and the friends heard Asha give out a big sigh.

"That bad, huh?" Daya said dryly. She never understood why Asha was so unhappy, especially lately. Her life seemed fine to her.

"Stop, Daya," Thania chided, as always playing peacemaker in their little threesome. "What's going on?" Thania repeated.

"Working at the nightclub is just…difficult. But I've told you that before."

Her two friends were silent. They'd heard this so often from Asha lately that they didn't know what to say to make things better for their friend.

"Then, get another job," Daya said, her constant refrain when this topic came up.

"It's not that simple, Daya," Asha said, her voice defensive now. "I can't just leave the nightclub, no matter how much I might want to."

"Well, how are things with David?" Daya said, referring to Asha's long-term boyfriend, and it was Thania's turn to sigh now.

Daya meant well most of the time, but she didn't know Asha like Thania did. Thania and Asha had been best friends since childhood, and there were certain things that Daya didn't know about Asha, even though they had grown to be very close, too. Plus, they were very different women—Daya was outgoing and used to pushing through whatever obstacle was in her path to get what she wanted, while Asha was more reserved and tended to accept her lot in life.

"David's fine," Asha replied softly, her voice tense. She continued, "Thania, tell us what the magazine people said when they called you to do the photo shoot," quite adeptly changing the subject.

Thania jumped in eagerly, deciding that changing the subject was indeed a good idea. "Well, the photographer for the magazine called me out of the blue a few days ago. I was totally shocked when she said the magazine wanted to do a follow-up with me, but this time with photos of me, as well."

A few months ago, Thania had landed an article in *Modeliste*, right before the debut of her very first fashion line. The article, combined with the coverage of her runway show, had catapulted Thania and her fashion line into the stratosphere. Suddenly, representatives of exclusive national stores were courting her, agents were trying to sign her, and she was attempting to keep sane while enjoying every moment of this newfound success.

"They want to know how I'm handling the sudden fame," she finished with a smile in her voice.

"Did you tell them you're handling it with lots and lots of wine?" Daya asked, and the three friends laughed again, breaking whatever tension had been there earlier.

"I figured that was a given," Thania said with another small laugh. "I have to get ready though, so this fabulously fun conversation with my girlfriends must end." Daya and Asha wished her luck and hung up.

* * *

Thania arrived at the photo shoot almost an hour early. She had showered and put on some soft, wide-legged cream-colored linen pants, and a white bohemian-style top. The assistant from the magazine had called earlier in the week to give her some final details about the shoot—she had said to dress comfortably, and not to wear any makeup.

For Thania, leaving the house without makeup was a serious fashion crime, so she already felt out of her element. But she had never modeled before so she was really quite nervous; her fashion line had been the center of attention for the last article. This time, she was the focus. Her thick gold bangles clinked together against her mocha-colored skin. She wore them everyday, almost like a security blanket.

A kick-ass, ridiculously expensive security blanket.

She pushed through the swinging doors of the magazine's headquarters, her Jimmy Choo sandals lightly slapping against the marble floor as she walked to the reception desk.

"May I help you?" The receptionist was dressed head-to-toe in Armani, and Thania wondered how much working at *Modeliste* paid.

"I'm Thania Walter, and I'm—"

"Oh!" The receptionist stood up immediately and continued, "Ms. Walter, it is such a pleasure to meet you!"

Well, this is...different.

The Armani-Girl was now around the receptionist desk and shaking Thania's hand as if she were meeting Diane Von Furstenberg. Thania's nerves were stretched thin by that point, and she hoped, for about the hundredth time, that everything went off without a hitch that afternoon.

The receptionist had left her post entirely and was escorting Thania to the photography studio. It was quite a walk, and the longer it took, the more anxious Thania grew.

"Here we are!" the Armani-Girl crowed, opening a door and swinging it wide, revealing an enormous room filled with people.

When Thania just stood wide-eyed in the doorway, the Armani-Girl gave her a discreet shove and told her to 'just hang out, someone will find you' before she closed the door and left.

Thania looked around the vast room, filled with lights and photography equipment and TV monitors. Off to the left were racks of clothes, and she was relieved to see a few racks from her fashion line among them. She had personally delivered them to the building earlier in the week, but had been fretting that somehow they wouldn't make it to the shoot.

Off to her right were models in various states of undress, being poked and prodded by makeup artists and hair stylists. Most of the models looked bored, but they were all so beautiful in their own unique ways.

As was her habit, she began to look each person over and evaluate what pieces from her line would look best on them. Her line wasn't designed for models —in fact, her clothes were meant to be worn by women with fabulous, real curves—but she was nervous enough that she began the ritual anyway.

That blonde would look incredible in the pencil skirt and cowl-neck blouse. The model with the beautiful caramel skin would look amazing in the burnt-orange dress with the plunge front. Let's see, who else is here? There's that guy over there being photographed right...now...holy shit...

Thania stared at the male model, unable to tear her eyes away. He was tall, with thick dark hair that was artfully styled to look messy, and even from this distance she could see that his eyes were the most gorgeous shade of green—like moss in a lily pond.

Okay Thania, get a grip. Really? Like moss in a lily pond?

She was still scolding herself when the man under her inspection turned and caught her staring. A shiver ran up her spine at the look on his face—he looked like he wanted to eat her with a spoon, and just for that moment, she didn't care about that because he had released her eyes from his hold in order to run his own gaze slowly down her body, seemingly cataloging every single curve she had. The shiver turned to a burn, and his gaze was like a physical touch. By the time he looked back up into her eyes, she felt as if he'd branded her.

What the hell is going on?

But she still couldn't pull her gaze away from him. Their eyes were locked in a sensual combat from fifty feet apart, and suddenly she wasn't aware of anything or anyone else in the room. He licked his full lower lip and her eyes darted there of their own volition. At that moment, someone near him called out, and he turned away, but not without quickly sliding his eyes down her body once more.

She stood there feeling let down somehow.

It was over before it had even begun.

"Hey, doll," a bright male voice said from behind her, and she turned to see a man dressed in a periwinkle silk shirt and extremely expensive black slacks, perusing her form.

She felt nothing when he did so, and briefly looked back at the male model, but he was busy taking instructions from the photographers. Feeling like she had lost something, she turned her attention to the man next to her.

"Are you Thania Walter? Never mind, I *know* who you are. I am Leonard Millis, but everybody calls me Len." He held out his perfectly manicured hand to her.

"Hi, Len. Yes, I'm Thania, and it's nice to meet you," she said as she grasped his hand tightly.

"A little uptight, doll?" he asked, as he pulled his hand away and shook it in the air.

"I'm sorry," she said, flustered. "I just...don't know what I'm doing."

Len had a kind expression on his face as he put his arm around her back and shoved her none-too-gently toward the makeup stations.

"You poor thing. You're a photo shoot virgin," he said straight-faced, and she laughed.

"Yes, I guess I am," she admitted as he pushed her into a chair facing a large mirror with bulb lights all around it.

"Don't worry, doll. I'll take it *nice and slow*," he said
with a good-natured smile, and she started to truly
relax.

She couldn't see the sexy model anymore, which
was good for her heartbeat and her libido. That was the
oddest thing that had happened to her in a while, and
in the world of fashion design that was saying
something. Len began by misting her face with a
cooling spray, telling her everything he was going to do
before he did it.

*Poor guy. I must be a hot mess for him to treat me with
such kid gloves.*

She listened with one ear to Len's chatter while her mind remained on the model.

"Do you know who that male model is?" she blurted out, interrupting Len's lecture on the importance of face primer and proper contouring shades. "Sorry," she said, embarrassment rolling over her like waves when Len didn't speak right away.

Great, I've made him go mute.

"You don't recognize him?" Len asked, mild disbelief in his tone, and Thania shook her head.

At that moment, the model moved into her view in the mirror and her heart sped up again.

"Who is he?" she practically whispered, even though the guy could not have possibly heard her from that far away.

"That is Vladislav Sakharov, doll," Len said, and she was stunned. He wasn't a model at all; he was a Russian jewelry magnate. He ran a world renowned jewelry empire, and she wondered why he was here of all places.

"I'm guessing from the look of shock on your face that you know who he is," Len said, as he added a smoky gray eye shadow onto her lid.

"Yes. I just…would never have thought he would be here," she said softly, watching Vladislav with one eye as he talked to the photographer.

"He is quite the delicious package, isn't he?" Len sighed and took a moment to stare at Vladislav himself, causing Thania to swat his arm. "Girl, *what* are you doing?" Len said, hitting her in the face with a makeup sponge.

"He's going to catch me, I mean *you*, staring," she whispered as she threw the sponge back and hit him on the nose.

Len laughed, the kind of laugh that made other people laugh just by hearing it, and Thania relaxed again when she couldn't hold back her smile. Len was

silent for a few minutes, highlighting her nose,

forehead, and Cupid's bow with a smirk on his face.

Thania chose to ignore him and keep watching

Vladislav in the mirror.

"He has got women chasing him around the globe,"

Len said in a warning tone.

"I'm sure he does."

"It is really quite sad, when you think about it. All

of these women thinking they have got a chance with a

gorgeous hunk of man-meat like him," he said with a

raised eyebrow.

"Shut up," she replied with no venom. But still, she watched Vladislav in the mirror.

"Did you know his last name means 'sugar' in Russian?"

"No, I didn't," she said, and she just knew that from now on anything related to sugar was going to make her think of him.

Great. He's famous and ridiculously rich, like a gazillionaire or something, he's got women from here to Timbuktu, and I can't stop staring. Get some self respect, Thania!

"You know that old song 'Pour Some Sugar on Me'?" Len asked, interrupting her musings.

"Yes…" she replied warily, afraid of where he was going.

"Well, he can pour his sugar on *me* anytime, doll," Len said, and Thania laughed loud enough to have a few people around them look over.

"I know exactly what you mean," she said with a smile.

* * *

She had been coiffed and plucked and stuffed into one of her own designs. She was ready. On the outside anyway. On the inside, she was a mess.

Vladislav had finished up and had disappeared behind the curtains of the changing area. She tried to pay attention to the photographer and the magazine's fashion editor, who were both giving her instructions.

"You are going to be great, Thania. Just act natural," the photographer said.

"We want you to be your authentic self," the editor said, and Thania nodded absently, wondering exactly what that meant. Her authentic self did not get coiffed and plucked and stuffed.

"Don't turn around," a gravelly male voice said from behind her, and without even looking, she knew it was him.

Even without his Russian accent, his voice would have been recognizable to her, as impossible as that sounded. She closed her eyes as the thrum of his voice sent a wave of heat pulsing throughout her body.

"I wish they had paired us together," he continued, so close now that his breath was hitting her hair.

She kept her eyes closed, not really capable of anything else at that moment. His body was so near that an invisible string seemed to be pulling her back toward him.

"You are exquisite," he said, his mouth practically touching her ear now, and she bit her lip hard to keep from making any noise.

She said nothing because she didn't know what to say. He backed off and she heard his footsteps as they took him further and further away. She took several deep breaths before she opened her eyes. The photographer and the editor were looking at her with renewed interest, and she turned to her right only to see Len smirking again from his makeup station.

"Sugar, doll!" he called out, making a show of taking a big drink from his coffee cup.

Thania rolled her eyes and fought to keep her head from floating off her shoulders and onto the ceiling.

* * *

Concentrating on the photo shoot after that encounter with Vladislav Sakharov was very difficult for Thania. She was dazzled, she could admit it, at least to herself. He was sexy and gorgeous, and he was so famous that most people knew his name. It was beyond flattering that he would seek her out like that.

But that still didn't explain her reaction to him. She kept replaying the whole thing over in her head—from the moment she had noticed him to the moment he had left. She was aware enough to do what the photographer and editor asked of her—'tilt your head, smile slightly, cross your legs'—but she wasn't really there in her mind.

In her mind, she was imagining what it would have been like if he had continued talking to her, and it made her cheeks flushed to the point that Len had to come over and powder her up a few times.

"Something got you hot and bothered, doll?" he said with a laugh the last time he'd come over.

She rolled her eyes at him. Oddly, she felt as if she had known Len forever, when she had only just met him that day.

"You did a great job, Thania!" the photographer said with a smile, and Thania was surprised it was over that quickly. It had all gone by in a blur once Vladislav had left.

"I hope some of them come out alright," she said, worried now that she hadn't given it her all, and it would show in the pictures.

"Oh, they'll be more than alright," the editor said. "You look stunning in the photos we've already seen."

She said goodbye, changed clothes, removed her makeup, and walked out the magazine's doors onto the sidewalk. She felt like a completely different person than she had when she'd walked through those same doors just a few hours earlier.

Chapter 2

Vlad

Vlad heard Maks talk, but he didn't really listen; his mind was back at the photo shoot from yesterday, thinking about the woman he had seen there. It seems that was all he had been doing since first laying eyes on her.

She was breathtaking. She wore gold bracelets, and they glinted against her skin like bronze in the sunlight. As soon as he saw her, he knew he had to have her. It was really that simple. He was used to getting what he wanted, but he wasn't sure how to find her.

"Vlad...Vlad!" Maksim Pelegin tried to get his attention, and Vlad swung his eyes toward the company's chief counsel.

"Sorry," Vlad murmured, still somewhat lost in thought.

"What has got you so distracted?" Vlad looked across the conference table at the man that asked the question, Mickhail Dvortsov, the heir to the jewelry empire.

These two men were the people he trusted most in the world, but something held him back from sharing his thoughts with them.

"We've discussed all of our business. In fact, I think it's time for a cocktail," Maks said, as he got up and walked over to the cherry wood bar built in to the corner of the conference room.

There was no need to ask what the other two men would be drinking—Maks reached into the specially designed chiller and pulled out a freezing bottle of Elit by Stolichnaya. He pulled three vintage Dyatkovsky crystal vodka glasses from the shelf and poured a generous amount in each. Careful not to clink the 200-

year-old crystal glasses against each other, he carried them back to the table, placing one in front of each of his friends. Finally, he sat down in his seat, pushing the Eames chair back so that he could relax and cross his legs.

The three men were used to the very best that life had to offer. None of them batted an eye at Maks opening yet another $3,000 bottle of vodka, or drinking it out of $500 crystal glasses made in the oldest factory in Russia.

"So, what is going on?" Mick asked once they had all pushed back from the table and gotten comfortable after a few sips of the vodka.

Vlad abruptly stood up and started to pace. Mick and Maks exchanged looks—neither of them had seen Vlad act like this before. Vlad finally stopped pacing and stood facing the floor-to-ceiling windows with his hands in his pockets. He looked at the darkened skyline, the tall buildings in the city beautiful at night, in a way that they weren't during the day. This was his favorite view since coming to America.

"There's a woman," he said in a low voice without turning around.

Maks laughed, and Vlad finally looked back.

"A woman has you pent up like this? Vlad, you turn women away every day."

"Yes, but not this woman. She was…ethereal." The other men just looked at Vlad, realizing that he was serious.

"Why don't you just ask her to dinner?" Mick asked, with a perplexed look on his face. So far, the other men could not see what the dilemma was.

"I can't. I don't know her name, or where she works. I don't know anything about her, really." Vlad slumped down into his chair again, unbuttoning his collar and loosening his tie before taking another sip of the vodka and sitting back.

"Where did you see her?" Maks asked, matching Vlad's serious tone.

"At the photo shoot yesterday."

"Well, if she is a model it should be easy to track her down. I'll call—"

"She's not a model. At least, I don't think she is."

"What was she doing there, then?"

"I don't know. It looked like she was going to be the subject of the shoot right after mine, but she did not have the look of a model. She was…I don't know…as soon as I saw her, I knew I had to speak to her, to see her up close."

Maks and Mick exchanged another glance; Vlad had never spoken about a woman with such a reverent tone.

Vlad ran one hand through his hair, causing the thick strands to stand up.

"I went up to her. I spoke to her. Her skin is the color of dark caramel, and when I came up behind her she smelled so sexy I did not trust myself to look directly into her eyes. And her *body*…so many beautiful curves, like a real woman should have. Not like these models I see everywhere." He stopped abruptly and took a large sip from the crystal glass.

The other two men were silent, listening to Vlad recite this woman's attributes.

"I can find her for you," Maks said after a few moments of silence.

"How?"

"I have my ways. Don't worry about how." Vlad narrowed his eyes at him.

"That sounds underhanded, Maks. I don't want to do anything that could be considered wrong, especially if she found out." Even as Vlad spoke the words, there was hope in his eyes.

"It's not underhanded, my friend. Just tell me everything you remember about her."

"I don't know…"

"Well, I *do*," Maks interrupted. "The Vlad Sakharov that *I* know has never pined for a woman before."

"I'm not pining…"

"Yes, you are," Maks interrupted him again. "I'll find out who she is, simply because I must see this magical creature that has brought my friend Vlad to heel."

Maks and Mick laughed, while Vlad said nothing, secretly hoping Maks actually could find her.

* * *

A half an hour later, Vlad's executive assistant Karen walked into his office, carrying a stack of papers and looking tired.

"What are you still doing here?" He asked her, surprised. It was almost eight o'clock, and Karen had a family.

"Just getting some extra work done but I'm leaving now," she said with a small smile, as she put the paperwork into the leather bin on his desk for him to read through at his leisure.

"Okay, have a good night then," he said, and she waved goodbye.

She was almost to the door when she turned around quickly. "Oh! I almost forgot. Maks asked me to give this to you before you left for the night."

He reached his hand out for the small piece of paper she was extending to him, not able to read what was on it from upside down. Just then the phone rang on his desk. Karen started to reach for it, but hesitated.

"Go home," Vlad told her, as he put the small paper inside his jacket pocket.

She waved again and was gone.

"Vladislav Sakharov," he said as he pressed the speaker phone button.

"Hello, my love." Vlad sighed and stood up, intending to refill his crystal glass at the built in bar. It was his ex-girlfriend, Irina.

"I'm not your love, Irina. In fact, I'm not your anything anymore," he said flatly as he poured a generous amount of Elit in his glass and took a strong swig.

"Oh darling, please don't be like that. I made one tiny mistake, and you've thrown me away," she said, her thick Russian accent even more pronounced when she used her little girl voice. That voice used to have an unfortunate effect on him; for two years she could get him to do almost anything if she used that voice.

But no longer.

"What do you want?" He settled in his chair behind his desk and started to sort through the stack of papers Karen had left for him in his leather bin.

"I want you, Vlad," Irina said, suddenly serious.

The little girl inflection in her voice was mysteriously gone. Vlad didn't respond; there really was not anything to say that hadn't already been said.

"We broke up six months ago, Irina," he reminded her.

"No, we didn't!" she yelled, and he realized that she was drunk again.

"Irina, I'm not doing this again."

"Doing what, Vlad? Staying in a relationship with the love of your life?"

Vlad laughed bitterly at her words, and this seemed to set her off even more.

"Don't laugh at me! You…you never appreciated me! I'm beautiful! I'm a famous model and I could have any man I want. I made *one mistake,* and you throw me away like trash!"

"I didn't throw you away, Irina. And it wasn't one mistake."

"I'm not perfect, Vlad, but you'll never have someone like me again. You'll regret the day you left me, and when you, do I won't…I won't be around to take you back."

"I'm sorry that you are in pain," he said, and he meant it.

He had cared deeply for Irina at one time, but her drinking had split them up even if she didn't want to admit she had a problem. He was done pretending everything was fine and then cleaning up her messes so no one would find out.

"Why won't you take me back?" she asked, the little girl voice back again.

Vlad sighed. "We both need to move on with our lives, Irina. It's been six months. I only want you to be happy."

"Well, if that was true, you would still be with me! Have I ever told you what an asshole you are?"

Yes, many times.

"I'm hanging up now, Irina."

"Don't you *dare* hang up on me! I swear Vlad, if you hang—"

He pressed the button to end the call and took a deep breath. He had stayed far too long in that relationship. The woman from the day before sprang into his mind again, and he smiled just thinking about her.

He shut things down for the day, and had almost reached the elevator before he remembered the small piece of paper in his pocket. He took it out and was amazed at what he read. Maks had done it.

Thania Walter

335 W. 89th Street

Chapter 3

Thania

God, those eyes…

Thania shook her head, annoyed at herself for yet again thinking about Vladislav. He had been in her thoughts, and unfortunately, in her dreams as well. She had woken up a little sweaty and a lot turned on, and she couldn't believe the effect one man was having on her.

While taking a shower, she wondered whether she should tell her best friends about him. She was meeting them for lunch in a little while. Daya would be excited but Asha would be reserved and most likely, a little concerned.

Especially if you tell them how you have basically been obsessed with him since first laying eyes on him yesterday.

She went to her closet and pulled out a pair of high waist black gaucho pants and a simple pink silk tank. The outfit emphasized her bust and her narrow waist, while camouflaging what she wanted hidden. The effect, especially after she wrapped a wide, fabric, multi-colored belt around her waist and knotted it, was an hourglass figure. *What woman doesn't want that*, she thought with a smile.

As she was putting on her makeup in the bathroom, she scolded herself yet again for thinking of Vladislav. She had far too much to do for her career to be daydreaming of happily-ever-after with a man she didn't even know. She had twenty minutes to get to the restaurant where she was meeting Asha and Daya, so she spritzed on her favorite perfume, put her gold bangles on her wrist, hung some chunky gold earrings from her ears, and added a few gold rings to her fingers. She grabbed her Valentino bag, slipped on her ballet flats, and was just about to open the door when the doorbell rang.

She looked through the peephole only to see two hands holding an enormous bouquet of red roses. Her heart pounded as she opened the door.

"Are you Thania Walter?" The young teenager looked like he could barely carry the bouquet—there had to be at least five dozen red roses in the vase.

"Yes, yes," she said as she waved the teenager inside and gestured toward a table for him to deposit it.

She grabbed some money out of her bag and tipped the boy before he left. All the while though, her sight was on the roses. She felt like her eyes were as big as saucers as she stared at it. She'd noticed almost immediately that there was a note peaking out from the beautiful stems, and she circled the table warily, hoping

beyond hope that they were from Vladislav, but almost

afraid to find out that they weren't.

Finally, she grabbed the thick envelope with her

name, 'Thania', written in bold, masculine script on the

front. She tore it open, only barely noticing the richness

of the stationery. It read:

> *Dear Thania,*
>
> *I apologize for tracking you down*
> *like this, but from the moment I saw*
> *you yesterday at the photo shoot, I*
> *needed to know who you are. You see,*
> *I work with beautiful jewelry, each*

piece exquisite and unique. You, my

darling Thania, possess these traits

as well.

I am an impatient man —when I

see something, or someone, that

piques my interest, I want more. And

I want to know more of you, Thania.

I would like to invite you to a

gala that the jewelry company is

throwing tonight. I am aware that it

is short notice, and that you may

have other plans. It is my hope that

you were as affected by me as I was

by you, and that you will be my

guest. I will send a car to pick you up

at 7 o'clock.

I hope to see you soon, my lovely

Thania,

Vlad Sakharov

Thania read the note twice, stunned. She sat down with the piece of paper in her lap, touching the soft as silk red rose petals with her fingertips as she looked at the blank wall across her apartment.

He calls himself Vlad. I like that. Oh my God, I have never had a man write such amazing words to me in my entire life. He's dangerous to my heart and my body, but right now I don't much care. I can't believe he went through

the trouble of finding me!

She put the note in her bag and ran out the door,

realizing that at that point she was going to be late to

meet Asha and Daya.

But what a story I have to tell them…

* * *

"Wait a minute! Vladislav Sakharov asked you

out?" Daya leaned across the table as she asked, her

eyes lit up with excitement.

"Yes," Thania replied with a small laugh. "That's what I have been trying to tell you both."

The three best girlfriends were eating brunch at their favorite downtown hotel-bar, the Hotelliere de Luxe. Asha ate her smoked salmon with avocado in silence; she'd barely said a word since Thania started to describe her interactions with Vlad.

"Where's the note?" Daya asked, still leaning forward, her spinach salad with cranberry vinaigrette forgotten.

"It's right here," Thania said, taking it carefully out of her bag.

Daya reached over and plucked it right out of her hand.

"Hey!" Thania objected, but soon gave up as Daya completely ignored her and read the note.

"Oh Lord, this man has some sexy handwriting," Daya murmured as she continued to look it over as if it held the secret nuclear codes or something.

"Can I have it back, please?" Thania asked with her hand out, and Daya reluctantly gave it to her.

"So, what do you think I should do?"

Both women looked back at her in silence.

"Girls!" she said with a laugh. "Come on, help me out!"

"Well, if he wants to take you somewhere, just be careful," Asha said, worry lines between her eyebrows.

"He *does* want to take her somewhere, Asha. He's asked her to go to a gala with him!" Daya responded, annoyance clear in her voice.

"Then just be careful when you go, Thania. I'm sure it will be fine," Asha said, her face devoid of any of the excitement that Daya's displayed.

Daya snorted and turned her back on Asha. "Forget her," she said to Thania, while Thania looked at Asha with concern. She definitely was not herself lately.

"What do *you* want to do?" Daya asked.

"I want to go, of course, but I don't know if I should."

"Let me get this straight. A gorgeous gazillionaire wants to take *you*, Thania Walter, to an A-list gala as his date, and you aren't sure if you *should*?" Daya was so worked up that she flagged down the waiter for another basket of bread.

"Well, that's exactly the problem. He *is* gorgeous, and he *is* rich, and he is *famous*," Thania said, making the word 'famous' sound dirty.

"So what?"

"I don't know if I'll fit in at that type of event."

"Of course, you will," Asha piped up, then went back to seemingly listen with just one ear.

The two other friends paused for a moment and looked at her, but that was all she wanted to say, apparently, so they turned toward each other again.

"You should go," Daya said bluntly. Then she just looked at Thania while she took a small bite of a roll.

"That's it? I should go?"

Thania was expecting more discussion, more dissection of every word in Vlad's note, more… something. It was as if her friends didn't really want to discuss it at all.

Something was going on with Asha that had nothing to do with Thania's dating life, this Thania knew. So, she was able to look past Asha's seeming disinterest because she was worried about her.

But Daya, she was acting a little envious. Not overtly so, just kind of annoyed that Thania would even think twice about whether to go to the gala with Vlad. It was as if Daya wasn't altogether happy for her. Thania knew that Daya's career and social life were not what she had envisioned for herself, but Thania also knew that both of those things would eventually work themselves out for Daya. She was gorgeous and kind, and those two attributes did not go together very often, so Thania was confident about Daya's future happiness. It seemed that Daya didn't feel that confident herself, though.

Deciding that the topic was now dead, Thania changed the subject. She asked about her friends' lives, getting caught up in the minutia that best friends share with each other. And if *she* listened with just one ear and responded enthusiastically at the right times, she couldn't really be faulted for daydreaming about the gala that night, could she?

* * *

Later that afternoon, Thania spent a lot of time getting ready for the gala. She wondered how she would find Vlad when she arrived; his note had said that he would send a car for her. The thought of seeing him again, and actually speaking to him this time, made her so nervous that she needed to sit down.

This is ridiculous. I might not even like him.

But somehow, Thania knew that would not be the case. She took a long bath, using some outrageously expensive exfoliating cleanser and body butter that she had received as a gift. Her skin was glowing like amber in the sun when she was finished. She didn't mess with her hair too much; she liked a natural look. She spent a lot more time on her makeup than she normally did.

She tried to remember Len's instructions from the photo shoot, and after a half an hour she sat back and smiled at the results. Her eyes looked bigger, her cheekbones more pronounced, and her lips were a gorgeous shade of burgundy that she had never worn before.

She slipped on a tiny pair of panties and walked to her closet. She knew exactly what she was going to wear. The dress was part of her own design collection —the finale in her next fashion show, to be exact. She had never had an opportunity to wear it before but she had been dying to. As soon as she read Vlad's note, she had thought of the dress. She pulled it from the back of her closet and hung it on a hook in her bedroom.

She unzipped the bag and pushed the sides apart. It was just as beautiful as she remembered. The dress looked deceptively simple. It was a dark navy silk, cut on the bias. It had one shoulder and from there it flowed down her body like an ocean hugs the sand. The bias cut started at the shoulder, and accentuated her breasts and hips while pulling in at her waist, giving her that hourglass figure she always sought out in her clothing. The hem reached the floor. But the real surprise was the tiny Swarovski crystals sewn here and there all over the dress, catching the light and creating

a glow that surrounded the lucky woman that wore it.

And tonight, that would be me.

Thania could not wear a bra with the dress—the

back was cut so low on one side that the very top of her

hip showed. It was simple but sexy as hell.

Before she slipped it on, she rubbed her entire body

with her favorite scented lotion and spritzed her

perfume liberally. It was a musky scent, and it

combined with her skin to create a lovely fragrance

unique to her. She loved it. She left off the gold bangles,

but put on a simple thin Swarovski bracelet and

matching stud earrings. The dress was the star of the show tonight.

At last, she was ready to slip on the dress. It was a quarter before seven o'clock, and she was so nervous that she needed to sit down again. She breathed deeply and looked at the dress where it still hung.

I can do this. Even if there is no attraction anymore, or he turns out to be a jerk, I can fake it for one evening.

Feeling more in control, she put the dress on and slipped on the custom made high heeled sandals that she had designed, as well. She had just tossed her phone, her slim wallet, and her lipstick into her clutch when the doorbell rang.

This is it. At least I'll have a few more minutes to gather

myself before I see Vlad at the gala.

Of course, the last thing she was expecting was to
see Vlad himself at the door.

Chapter 4

Vlad

Vlad could barely think after she opened the door. She took his breath away, quite literally.

She can't be real.

Even though he knew it was incredibly rude, he said nothing and let his eyes wander slowly down from her face to her pretty toes peeking out from her dress. By the time he had wandered back up again, she was smiling shyly at him.

"I'm so sorry," he said. "I did not mean to be rude. It's just…your beauty is beyond words. I can't believe you're real," he admitted to her.

Her smile widened as she moved back to let him inside her apartment. He walked in slowly, surreptitiously glancing around as she closed the door behind him.

Roses aren't good enough for this woman.

He took some deep breaths to gather his composure. He carried a single flower with him, and should have already given it to her before he had stepped over the threshold. This was new territory for him, being swept away by a woman. He didn't know what to do or how to act.

"Would you like a drink?" she asked, and her voice hit his ears like the smooth taste of his favorite vodka sliding down his throat.

It was the first time he had heard it, and it fit her well. It was sexy, without trying. He turned toward her and stopped, stunned once more. He watched her back as she walked into her kitchen, separated from the living room by an island. He started to walk toward her—he did not think first before moving. He was behind her in the small kitchen after taking about six steps, and now it was her turn to stop what she was doing. She did not turn around, but he could hear her uneven breathing as he stood behind her in the small space.

His heart pounded as he stared at her back. The dress plunged from one shoulder all the way to her hip, exposing her entire back and hinting at the swell of her ass. Her skin was absolutely perfect. It looked so soft that he ached to touch it. But he didn't trust himself. So he lifted the single white orchid that he had brought for her, and touched the nape of her neck with it.

"What are you—"

"Shhh…" he said softly as he slowly, and very gently, dragged the flower down the bare skin of her back. He saw goose bumps break out on her arms, and his dick swelled.

"Vlad," she breathed when he reached the small of her back, and the sound of her voice saying his name made it almost impossible to stop from turning her around.

Take it easy. Don't scare her.

So he said nothing, but continued the orchid's descent, finally skimming the flower over the forbidden skin she had exposed. By then, her voice, the smell of her skin, the look of her luscious body in that dress had all combined so that he was rock hard and extremely uncomfortable. But he was a gentleman. He would wait for her.

"A flower for you, Thania," he said in his gritty voice, and she finally turned around.

They were so close now that he could see her eyes were not as dark as he had originally thought; they were caramel with flecks of gold. He handed her the orchid.

"You are the most exquisite woman I have ever seen," he told her seriously, and she stared up at him, seemingly as enamored of him as he was of her.

"Thank you," she said softly.

Vlad was unclear if she was thanking him for the flower or the compliment. It did not matter, he thought, as he continued to stare at her.

"Shall we go?" she asked, and he stepped back immediately.

There would be time alone later.

* * *

"Edward, have you met Thania Walter?"

Vlad watched as Thania turned and smiled at the man he introduced to her, answering gracefully 'fashion designer' when Edward asked her profession.

"Well, if you are here with Vlad, then you must be a great designer," Edward replied, and he handed her his business card. Surprised, she glanced down at it. It read: *Edward Bancroft III, President, Bancroft Department Stores*.

"It is a pleasure to meet you, Edward," she replied with a smile.

Vlad didn't plan to introduce her to the head of the country's largest, and most posh, department store chain, but when Edward walked by, he figured it was a great idea.

"Send some samples of your work to the address on the card," Edward instructed her.

"Of course, of course," she said.

"Just send a note that it is from you. I'll make sure it gets to the right people," he said kindly, and then he shook her hand and then Vlad's, before stepping away.

"Thank you so much," she belatedly said to his back.

Vlad had watched the entire exchange from beside her, and could not help but be impressed with her composure.

"Oh my God!" she exclaimed, as soon as Edward was out of earshot. She placed the business card in her clutch, and then pressed a hand to her burning cheeks.

Vlad laughed and handed her a glass of Cristal champagne.

"I cannot believe you introduced him to me like he was your neighbor or something!" She said, and he laughed again. She took a sip of her champagne and looked around at the glitz and glamour of the gala.

"Well, actually, he is..."

"...your neighbor," she interrupted him, her voice dry. And then she laughed out loud, a deep, rich laugh that made him smile just from hearing it.

She is so beautiful. And the way she handled Edward just now...

Vlad was amazed at the way Thania had handled all of the introductions he'd thrown at her in the last two hours. She was a consummate professional, a smart businesswoman, and he was surprised that he was even more intrigued by her after he had watched her interact with the dignitaries, diplomats, and captains of industry that had attended the gala. To him, they were all just regular people. But to every woman he had dated in the past, those same people had been ways to get themselves in the society pages.

At the last event he had brought his ex Irina to, she had spent the entire night in front of the camera. Tonight, Thania had rejected any opportunity to be in a photo, and with the press in attendance, the chances were myriad. But she had wanted nothing to do with that, and had concentrated on him instead.

Thania was definitely impressed with the people he had introduced her to. Who wouldn't be? But she treated the wait staff with the same respect that she had spoken to an oil magnate, and it was wonderful for Vlad to witness. The women in his past, especially Irina, all had treated the wait staff as second class citizens. Thania was different than any woman he had ever taken out before—she was intelligent, business savvy, confident, and respectful to everyone.

As far as he could tell, she was perfect.

* * *

"The orchid looks lovely in your hair," he said as they stood in a corner of the gala and drank champagne.

"Thank you," Thania replied softly, as she looked into his eyes.

Tension was there between them suddenly, thick and pulsing with awareness of each other. Since they had left her apartment three hours earlier, they had been surrounded by crowds and unable to talk alone. He had watched people, men and women, regard her with frank interest, and he was proud to have her on his arm. But if he'd had a choice, he would have been right there in the corner with her for the entire three hours.

Thania touched the flower behind her left ear. Before they had left her apartment, she had cut the stem and tucked it into her hair. Vlad felt almost overwhelmed by the sweetness of the gesture, and he couldn't believe how sentimental he had become. He wasn't a sentimental man. But he had realized earlier that he was when it came to Thania, and it did not scare him. He only felt anticipation when he thought of learning more about her, and spending more time with her.

"Thank you for asking me to come with you," she said, their gazes locked.

"Of course, of course," he replied, gently mimicking her response to Edward Bancroft earlier, and they both laughed. He reached out and brushed his fingers against her neck, and she shivered.

I want her.

"I've had such a wonderful time with you tonight, Thania. I am so glad you came with me."

"This has been the strangest experience," she said after a pause.

"How so?"

"We met in a very odd way. Well, we didn't even *meet*, really. And now here we are, and the night has been so memorable, and I'm just…happy."

"I'm happy too, Thania," he replied.

The gala had started to wind down; they could slip out and no one would notice.

I wonder if she will come to my home if I ask her. I need to touch her, feel her underneath me.

He moved closer to her, and their bodies brushed together. Liquid fire raced straight to his dick. The smell of her skin enveloped him like a delicious fog, and he inhaled deeply. He glanced down and noticed that her nipples were hard through her dress and he just barely stopped himself from reaching for them.

"Vlad," she whispered against his neck, and he gently pushed her into the corner so that his body caged her in.

"I want to be alone with you," he told her softly, his stiff erection brushing against her stomach.

She moaned so low that he could barely hear her, but even so, it was like a siren's song to him. He wanted to hear her moan again. He wanted to *make* her moan.

"Come home with me," he said, his mouth against her hair.

"Yes," she whispered, and he immediately took her hand in order to turn around and leave.

"You cheating pig!" a woman screamed from behind them, and people from all over the gala stopped to stare.

He turned around to face the woman, knowing before he did so that it was Irina. He would recognize that angry screech anywhere. Thania attempted to pull her hand free, but he held firm.

"Stop it, Irina," he said loudly, annoyed beyond words that she had interrupted his time with Thania.

"Who is this whore that you're with?" Irina sneered, and Thania gasped beside him.

Curiosity had caused a crowd to form, and he pushed Thania behind him.

"Don't *ever* call her that word again!" he thundered, and it was clear that Irina did not expect that reaction from him.

Thania hung back behind him, but he knew she must be mortified.

"You and I are *not* together anymore, Irina," he said slowly, as if he spoke to a child.

"That's not—"

"Yes, it *is* true," he interrupted loudly. "We broke up six months ago." He felt Thania relax slightly against his back, but this conversation wasn't ending quickly enough for him. "It has been over for a long time, Irina. Stop calling me. Stop harassing me. And stop embarrassing yourself in public," he said as he noticed her swaying slightly.

She was drunk again.

He turned back to Thania and grasped her hand gently. She looked up at him with humiliation in her eyes, and he hated that Irina had caused it. He turned and started to walk through the mass of people that gathered, pulling Thania's hand, and they parted to let them through. Just as they got to the edge of the crowd, Irina was there again, and before he knew it, she had tossed her full glass of scotch at Thania's dress.

"Oops," Irina said as she smiled and swayed.

The crowd murmured all around them, but Thania said nothing. She just looked down at her gown as if in a trance.

"Get out!" he yelled at Irina, and just like that, security guards were there to escort her away.

She could be heard laughing and singing as she got closer to the exit.

"Thania," he said gently, hoping that she would look at him.

But when she did look up, he almost wished that she hadn't; the only thing in her eyes was devastation.

"Are you okay?" he asked as he gathered up some linen napkins from the surrounding tables in an attempt to help her clean up.

"It's ruined," she whispered, and he stopped. "It's my design. It's a one of a kind, and it's supposed to be the finale in my show next month."

He crumpled the napkins in his hands and swore. "I am so sorry, Thania," he said, horrified at what Irina had done. "Irina, she just…is having trouble moving on. It's nothing, I swear," he pleaded, worried that Thania would no longer want to date him. "I'm sure we'll never see her again after this public display. She will never be invited anywhere again."

I will make sure of it.

Thania took a deep breath and settled her shoulders, her head held high.

"It's fine," she said in a clear voice, and he was so proud of her in that moment. She took the napkins from him and dabbed at her dress until the worst was mopped up.

"I'm sorry," he said again, and she surprised him by wrapping her arms around his neck. Quickly, he gathered her as close as possible.

"You don't need to apologize for her behavior," she said into his ear.

"I know, but—"

"No buts. You are not responsible for her, and I'm not going to allow her to ruin what has been a wonderful night."

His heart raced at what he thought she was saying.

"Besides," she continued softly, her words tickling his neck, "You came to my rescue. It was quite gallant. I know I'm a modern woman and should not need a man to rescue me, but it felt very nice nonetheless." She snuggled her face into his neck, and he reflexively pulled her tighter to him.

She was amazing, absolutely amazing.

"Will you come home with me?" he dared to ask her again, his heartbeat erratic as he waited for her answer.

They were still in a tight embrace, their hearts beating against each other. After what felt like a very long time, she whispered one word.

"Yes."

Chapter 5

Thania

She usually did not go home with men on a first date. It just wasn't her style. But Vlad was different, and Thania didn't want the night to end yet. So she had accepted Vlad's invitation, and after that it became a bit of a blur.

Vlad took charge and escorted her to ladies' room so she could clean up a bit. When she was finished, he had been waiting in the hallway, tapping away on his phone, looking so dashing in his tuxedo that her stomach twisted.

When he had looked up at her and smiled, her *heart* had twisted.

I'm in trouble.

But still, she went with him, knowing that every moment she spent near him, her feelings for him would increase. It was the strangest sensation—she had never felt this drawn to a man before, as if an invisible rope linked them. It was chemistry. How else could she explain her extreme attraction to him?

Vlad had gathered up her wrap from the coat check, and had arranged for his car to be brought out front. He had insisted that she stay inside until the car arrived, telling her that he was concerned she would be cold. She thought it was a little heavy handed, but sweet nonetheless. She knew that his intention was only to make her more comfortable after their encounter with Irina.

Don't think about it—do not let her in to ruin the rest of your night with Vlad.

He had paid the parking attendant and held the door to the passenger side for Thania himself, making sure that she managed the dress and her heels, which was no small feat considering his car was a Porsche 911. The tiniest, but most luxurious car she had ever been inside.

Once Vlad had settled in behind the wheel, it had felt as if they were in a cocoon together. He had been right there, his arm grazing hers as he had shifted gears. It wasn't even his skin touching her, it was his dress shirt; but even so, the feeling of the soft brushed cotton against her skin had sent tingles racing up her arm.

The car's leather passenger seat had molded itself to her body, leaving her to feel so relaxed that she had almost fallen asleep on the twenty minute ride to his home.

Thania knew that going to his home might mean something would happen between her and Vlad that night. Normally, she would never do something like that, but her reactions to Vlad had been anything but normal up to that point. Why put an artificial barrier between them? She had decided to enjoy his company, and to just follow her feelings on the subject. Besides, she had known without question that Vlad would be a perfect gentleman.

Well, hopefully not a 'perfect' gentleman.

They had finally reached his home, after not speaking much during the drive. But it had been a comfortable silence, as if they had known each other for years, and she hadn't felt the need to force conversation.

Vlad had pulled up a long driveway and parked in the circular drive outside of an enormous white house. A mansion, really, with so many gabled windows and at least a couple of wings, that she could not make them all out in the dark.

This isn't awkward at all.

Suddenly, she felt a bit out of place, when up until that moment she had been completely comfortable. Obviously, she had known that Vlad had money. He ran one of the most exclusive jewelry businesses in the world, attended galas on a semi regular basis, drove a Porsche, and he even *looked* rich, in the way that only a person born into wealth could achieve. But this—his house—had been a bit much for her to absorb. She stood staring at the gigantic home for at least a full minute, all the while clutching the open passenger door.

"Thania? Are you alright?"

She turned toward Vlad, who stood next to her, an expression of concern on his beautiful face. And the memory of how he had defended her from Irina had made her defenses crumble faster than they had come up in the first place.

What did it matter how much money he had? I can't judge him for having money. That's as bad as judging someone for not having it.

So, she took his outstretched hand, and they walked up the wide stone steps into the house. It was lit up like it was Christmas morning inside, with what appeared to be every light switched on. She noticed that there was a direct view from the front door, all the way to the back of the house and out the floor-to-ceiling back windows, and she caught a hint of the rolling hills just beyond.

The view must be spectacular in the morning. Maybe I'll find out.

Vlad offered to get some clothes for her to change into, since her gown was covered in sticky, warm scotch. Luckily, none of what Irina had tossed on the gown had hit Thania's skin, but even so, she'd been wanting to get out of the dress the entire ride to Vlad's home.

She followed him down one of the hallways that stretched off the enormous foyer like the spokes on a wheel. He stopped outside of a room with double doors and pushed one open before gesturing her inside with his hand.

It was his bedroom, and she found herself momentarily unable to move. It was rich, with deep, masculine colors on the walls, floor, and the bed itself. But still, it felt open and inviting, like Vlad himself.

Most significantly, it smelled like him. That was what made her stop before entering his bedroom. It was as if Vlad's unique and sexy scent was multiplied by one hundred, and she was already practically a puddle when she smelled his scent from him alone.

He walked over to one of his dressers, opening and closing them while she looked all around the bedroom suite. He cleared his throat and she swung her head toward him, only to find herself caught snooping with her eyes. She laughed and so did he, before he handed her a pile of soft clothing.

"I think this might be more comfortable for you to wear than your dress," he said as he gazed at her dreamily.

She found that she was unable to tear her eyes away from him to look down at the clothes, so she thanked him, and he closed the door behind him as he left her alone.

After a few moments of simply standing there, she looked down and saw that he had given her a pair of his own sweatpants and a huge t-shirt to wear. They were both so soft that when she finally pulled them on, she breathed a sigh of relief. She hadn't been aware until that moment how uncomfortable the ruined dress had been to wear.

The only problem with his choice of clothing was that she wasn't wearing a bra. So with the t-shirt being so big on her, it fell off one-shoulder no matter how she adjusted it, and her breasts were now untethered and *right there*. She reasoned that there wasn't much she could do to change it, and she was so much more comfortable that she couldn't bare the thought of stepping back into the stained gown.

When she walked back down the hallway slowly— in order to make sure that she found her way to the center of the spoke—she saw Vlad stop and stare at her.

She looked down—she had been forced to roll the waist of his sweatpants down and the legs up—and she wasn't sure what he was thinking. But the look in his eyes was slightly predatory, especially when he noticed the t-shirt, and what was happening underneath it. He cleared his throat and quickly turned away, then invited her to get comfortable.

* * *

So that was how she found herself in his living room now, with Vlad in the kitchen, while she quite blatantly checked out his home. Or what she could see of it, anyway.

Vlad was truly unlike any other man she had dated, or even met before. She wasn't used to such kindness from men. Not to mean that she had allowed herself to be mistreated, of course, but the level of caring Vlad showed toward her tonight was eye-opening. He had made sure that she was comfortable the entire evening, that her drink was always filled, that her food was warm and plentiful, and that she was enjoying herself by introducing her around. He seemed proud to have her on his arm, and she had to admit that it was a nice feeling to be there.

There were some people there that might have said she didn't belong—that she had not achieved the level of success necessary to be at such an event. But Vlad, and the people he had chosen to introduce her to—all highly respected in their fields—apparently thought she was a wonderful addition to the guest list.

She had to admit, it felt really nice to be doted on. That wasn't a particularly popular opinion, when women were working so hard to advance up the ranks of business, and be viewed as equals. But she truly believed that Vlad *did* view her as an equal; his wonderful treatment of her, and his respect for her as a businesswoman, were not mutually exclusive.

"Please, get comfortable," he had told her before he'd disappeared into the kitchen.

Wearing his extremely soft and luxurious clothes, getting 'comfortable' was not a problem. So she padded barefoot around his large living room, and admired his modern art collection.

This is truly amazing.

He had quite an eclectic collection. She was not an expert by any means, but she recognized a few pieces by some up and coming artists. He had an original painting by Sebastian Lloyd Rees on his wall, directly next to a few professionally framed crayon drawings, obviously from a child's hand. The colorful drawings all had a similar note written on them: 'To Uncle Vlad, I miss you! Love, Tati'. Her heart melted a little bit more.

All I need is a puppy to come bounding into the room right now, and I'm a complete goner.

"Those are from my niece, Tatyana," Vlad said from across the room, causing her to turn and look at him.

He had taken off his tuxedo jacket and cummerbund, and rolled up the sleeves of his white dress shirt. His tie had been loosened as well, and if it was possible, he looked even more gorgeous to her than he had at the gala.

"I see that," she replied with a smile, turning back to the drawings again.

"Where does she live?"

"She's in St. Petersburg, Russia, with my brother, Viktor and his wife, Eugenia. She's my favorite of all of my nieces," he admitted with a smile as he placed the small tray he was carrying on to the coffee table in front of the fireplace.

"How many nieces do you have?" she asked as she walked closer to him and sat down on the plush couch in front of the coffee table.

He hesitated as he crouched down in front of the fireplace to put wood, kindling, and some newspaper, in order to start a blaze.

"Only one," he said with a wry smile, and she laughed.

"How often do you see your family?" she asked while they both watched his fire start to burn, and quickly settle into a cozy blaze.

"I get back to Russia a minimum of six times per year," he replied as he sat down next to her.

The couch was so plush, and she'd tucked her feet under her, that his weight caused her to sway toward him. She reached out and put her hand on his arm to stop from completely falling into his lap, and just like that, the intense sexual awareness of each other was back. Not that it had ever really gone away, but now, as she clutched his muscular bicep and stared into those green eyes, it was almost impossible to pull back. She did pull back, however, since she didn't want to come off as too aggressive.

He's from another culture. Maybe he'll think less of me if he knew what I'm thinking.

So she sat back, and he visibly relaxed. The comfortable silences of before had been replaced by awkward, stilted moments.

"Six times a year? That's wonderful," she said, hoping to ease the stiffness between them, even by just a small amount.

"Yes, and my family comes here, as well. So, all in all, we see each other fairly frequently. But out of everyone in my family, Tati actually *is* my favorite," he said, his smile so wide that the power of his dimples was released on her.

Oh God, he's got dimples.

"What about you?" he asked as he offered her a glass of red wine from the tray in front of them.

She took it and sipped, the expensive goblet feeling heavy in her hand. "I only get to Russia every six or seven years," she joked, and he laughed.

He leaned back into the couch, his weight messing with her center of gravity again. He reached out, and his hand landed on her naked shoulder to steady her, but this time he didn't remove it.

"I meant, what about *your* family? Tell me about them."

His gritty voice, his damned framed children's drawings, and his fingers, which were now gently exploring the top of her shoulder, all combined to make answering him right then almost impossible. She took another fortifying sip of the delicious wine.

"Well, let's see. I grew up in New York City, and my parents still live there. I see them only a few times a year, but we speak often. I have just one sibling, my brother, Darren. He's finishing up a degree in photography at the Art Institute of Chicago in a few months."

He listened intently while she spoke, but he never stopped touching her shoulder. In fact, his fingers were starting to slowly creep down her arm. Tingles shot down to her hand, and she almost felt like shaking it to wake it up from falling asleep—the feeling was the same and just as intense. But she stayed right where she was.

"The Art Institute? That is quite a good program, I hear," Vlad said, looking impressed.

"Yes, well my parents are both doctors. So, when I announced I was going into fashion design, and a couple of years later, Darren began studying at the Art Institute, I think they were a bit dismayed."

"But, why?" Vlad asked, genuinely perplexed.

"Because they were worried that the two of us would end up being starving artists," Thania said with a laugh, and Vlad's eyes crinkled up at the corners, causing her breath to catch.

"I guess they don't have to worry about that with you anymore, do they?" he responded, seeming not to notice her quickened breathing.

"No, I guess not," she admitted softly, trying desperately not to embarrass herself by allowing her attraction to him to show.

He was still caressing her arm, and it felt so good that her panties were already wet, but he seemed as unaffected as a statue.

"Are you permanently in America?" she asked, partly to fill the silence, but mostly because she needed to know the answer.

"Yes and no," he replied, and she raised an eyebrow at him, causing him to laugh again. "I know, it's vague. The truth is, I'm not sure. I will be here for the next couple of years establishing our expansion into the U.S. market. But after that is completed, and the U.S. stores are stable, I will most likely head back to Russia."

His eyes looked wary now, while at the same time her heart sank. He would be leaving at some point, even if in the distant future, so no matter what happened between them, it wouldn't be life changing.

Even though it already feels that way.

She responded appropriately, but later she could not remember what she'd said. They continued to chat and drink wine in front of the fire, while another part of her mind was absorbing what he had told her, and what it meant.

At least he was being honest and upfront, she thought. He wasn't trying to lead her on by giving her hope of a long-term relationship. It was clear to her from what he'd said, that he wasn't looking for a commitment, or even a simple relationship with her. Added to that, the fact that he had just recently ended things with Irina, it was no wonder he didn't want anything serious.

She actually appreciated his honesty, because it made things so much simpler for her. She knew exactly where she stood with him, and any decisions she made about tonight would be free of any hope or longing on her part. She could choose to be with him tonight, without wondering what it might mean for their future —because there wouldn't be one.

He seemed to be watching her even more warily now, no doubt wondering what she was thinking. She smiled at him and leaned her head down so that her cheek brushed the back of his hand on her shoulder. He stopped moving and just watched her, passion and lust combining like an inferno in his eyes.

She lifted her hand and slipped it behind his neck, and his skin was taut and hot, but silky to her touch. She raised her head and he closed his eyes, as her fingers gently caressed his nape.

Her name escaped his lips on a sigh, *"Thania."* He opened his eyes, and she was right there, only inches away. His breath hit her face like the steam from a shower, laced with the scent of mint, red wine, and Vlad himself.

She was trembling now and hoping that he would take over at some point. She figured she had made it pretty clear by then what she wanted. It didn't matter that there was no future between them—if all she could ever have was one night with him, she would take it.

He finally leaned forward the two inches necessary to kiss her, and she moaned deep in her throat at the feeling of his plump lips against her own. He used his strong arms to lift her up and place her on his lap sideways, never breaking the kiss. She ran her hands up and over his shoulders, feeling his muscles twitch and flex at her touch. Her own body was humming from the contact with him, and she couldn't even imagine how amazing having sex with him would be.

He gently pushed his tongue between her lips, and suddenly, she felt nothing else but his mouth on hers. Her legs, her arms, her fingers, they were all numb, as his soft tongue swept through her mouth. He savored her lips as if she were a delicious piece of candy, licking every corner and sucking on her tongue softly. It was the most sensual, erotic kiss she had ever received, and it seemed to affect him deeply as well, judging by the very hard erection pressing against her thighs where she sat on him. Just by that kiss, everything was crystal clear to her.

I don't care about tomorrow. I'll take him now, for tonight, and that will be enough.

Chapter 6

Vlad

He had been holding back all night from touching her, but he simply could not do that any longer. When he saw her in his sweatpants and t-shirt, her body practically swallowed up by the material, he thought she was even sexier than she was in her gown. If that was even possible.

Then, he noticed that she wore no bra under the t-shirt and he'd had to turn away quickly, to avoid her seeing his rigid cock. He stood in the kitchen, gathering the wine and the goblets, and telling himself to get control.

He couldn't just take what he wanted from her—which was her naked and writhing underneath him, while she moaned his name—he had to wait for the right time. And he realized that just because she had agreed to come to his home with him, it did not necessarily mean that she wanted to sleep with him. It was important to him that she not feel pressured; if they slept together, he wanted her to have zero regrets about it in the morning.

That was how he already knew he would feel after they slept together, if they ever did. He was certain he wanted Thania for the long term, maybe even forever, and he was willing to take whatever time she needed in order for her to feel the same way about him.

He had so enjoyed talking with her about his family and his niece, and hearing about her own family. Those were the details he wanted to know about her—he wanted to know all of the events in her life that had occurred before they had met.

As they sat on the couch, sipping wine and talking, a constant refrain was flowing through his mind:

She is entrancing.

She was so, so beautiful, as she smiled and laughed with him. Her sense of humor was infectious, and her intelligence was, as far as he could see, without bounds. But there, in the back of his mind at all times, was his awareness of her as a woman. There was no way to explain why someone could be attracted physically to one person but not another. It was that elusive word—chemistry—that was simply there, or it was not.

He was attracted to her, more so than he could ever remember being with another woman. She consumed his thoughts, and he was trying so desperately to be a gentleman around her.

But when they were on the couch together, and she kept falling into him, he'd touched her shoulder to steady her, and he simply was unable to remove his hand. She didn't seem unhappy with the situation, so he had started to stroke her silky skin, his fingers seeming to vibrate like a tuning fork as he touched her. He tried to concentrate on their conversation after that, but it had become nearly impossible. Every cell in his body wanted her—wanted to touch her, smell her, taste her, lick her, and yes, make love to her. He knew he was not going to be able to sit next to her for much longer.

And then she put her head down on his hand, so that the backs of his fingers touched her delicate cheek. There was nothing he could do to stop after that, no matter how hard he tried. She slipped her hand behind his neck, and his heart rate went through the roof. Her tiny fingers felt so good, so right, on the back of his neck, that he involuntarily closed his eyes. It was the only way he could prevent himself from pouncing on her like a wild animal. Even so, one word escaped his lips without his volition.

"*Thania.*"

He opened his eyes then, hoping he hadn't scared her away. But she was right there, her beautiful face only inches away, looking at him steadily. He felt her tremor as she watched him, and he lost the fight.

He leaned in and kissed her. A kiss should be simple. It should be two mouths coming together in preparation for the future act—the actual lovemaking itself. But not this kiss. Not with Thania. No, this kiss was *the* kiss he would remember for all of his life—he knew it as soon as his lips met hers.

The feelings that rushed throughout his body as they kissed were unlike any he had felt before, with anyone else. He was consumed by the kiss, and within seconds, his body was on fire. He grabbed her up from next to him and set her on his lap, but never was he willing to let go of her mouth.

She opened to him like a flower in the sun, and when his tongue touched hers, the feeling bordered on ecstasy. He wasn't going to come, but his dick was as hard as concrete, and he tried not to rub it against her buttocks as she sat on him.

Normally, when he kissed a woman, it was simply the prelude to other things. It was pleasurable, of course, but he was always anticipating what was to come.

He could have kissed Thania all night. She went limp in his arms, her soft breasts pushed up against his chest, and her luscious ass resting on his engorged cock. He tilted her head to the side so that he could kiss her deeper—it was as if he couldn't get enough of her mouth. Her lips were so soft, her mouth tasted like honeysuckle, and her tongue was hot and quick to tangle with his. He kissed her for a long time, and frankly, he never wanted to stop.

But his dick had other plans. At some point, his mind shut down, and his cock took over. He needed her naked. He pulled away from the kiss, barely able to catch his breath.

"Will you come with me to my bedroom, Thania?" he asked, his voice unrecognizable to him. He watched from two inches away as her eyes darkened to milk

chocolate, and he noticed that her face was flushed,
and her lips, swollen.

I did that to her.

He said it to himself like he was a caveman, but
nonetheless, a feeling of pride spiked through him at
the evidence of her reaction to him. He waited for what
seemed like minutes, but was probably only a few
seconds, for her to respond.

"Yes, Vlad. Yes," she breathed into his mouth, and
they were kissing again.

He stood up with her in his arms, without breaking
the kiss, even though he wasn't sure his legs would
actually cooperate since his entire body was tingling.

But he managed it, and she clamped her arms around his neck as he walked by memory to the foyer, and down the hallway.

Once they got to the closed double-doors of his bedroom, he gently placed her on the floor and held her up as he twisted one knob. He had to stop kissing her then, and it physically pained him to do so. But Thania had other plans, apparently. He managed to get the door open, and then she was on him, using her hands to push him up against the wall in the hallway. Surprised, he let her have her way, since really, why would he complain about that?

She stood on tiptoe and kissed him again, and he put both arms around her back and gathered her up tight. Soon, their tongues were in a battle that both of them would win, and she was running her hands up and down his back. She pulled his dress shirt out of the back of his pants and the second that her fingers first touched the skin of his lower back, he pulled away from her mouth with a hiss.

Holy shit.

Her touch felt like an electrical current was flowing directly from that spot, straight to his dick. It was unexpected, and he needed a moment to wrap his brain around this level of sexual synergy. Once he did, approximately one millisecond later, he squeezed her body tighter with his arms and lifted her off the ground.

He turned her around so that *he* was pushing *her* up against the wall. He flattened her against the wall and grabbed her hands in his own. Lacing their fingers together, he kissed and sucked on her neck as he held her hands above her head. She moaned and parted her thighs for one of his legs to intrude, and his dick swelled even more.

He kissed her mouth again and released her hands. He sucked on her tongue as he ran his hands down the front of her t-shirt. Well, *his* t-shirt. He felt her large breasts for the first time through the shirt, and Thania practically became boneless. The only thing holding her up at that point was his leg between hers.

He quickly ran his hands down and then back up, under the hem of the t-shirt, gliding the tips of his fingers over her soft, quivering stomach. He would give her love bites on her stomach later, but at that moment, he was a man on a mission.

When he finally cupped her breasts in his hands, Thania immediately broke the kiss and let her head fall back to rest on the wall. He squeezed her softly and watched her face as she closed her eyes and bit her lip. Their faces were very close, they were breathing the same air, and when he pinched her nipples gently, she moaned and then grabbed his forearms tightly.

He pushed her breasts together with his hands, and she ground her pussy against his leg. She pulled her head away from the wall and kissed him again, as she rubbed harder against him. He could feel that her pussy was wet all the way through her sweatpants and his dress pants, the heat of her core making his head swim.

He pulled his mouth away from hers, and she audibly protested. But he needed to see and taste her right that minute. He pulled the t-shirt up and she raised her arms up to help him ease it off her. When he saw her for the first time, he was so stunned he just stared at her without even tossing the t-shirt to the floor.

"Vlad?" Thania asked in a sexy-as-hell, raspy voice.

"I can't believe you even let me touch you...you are the most gorgeous woman I have ever seen," he told her, as his eyes seared hers with his intensity.

A beautiful rosy flush bloomed on her neck and down her chest at his words, and he leaned down to suck one nipple into his mouth, tossing the shirt aside as he did so.

"*Oh God,*" Thania groaned, his mouth causing her body to shake.

She reached up with both hands and pulled his head closer to her, more for balance than anything else. His tongue pressed her erect nipple into the roof of his mouth, and then he sucked hard. He moved to her other breast, and she whimpered from the pleasure. Still sucking on her nipple, he leaned down and put one arm behind her knees and one arm behind her back, and picked her up.

He placed her on the bed and stood up. She watched him from underneath half-closed lids as he started to remove his shirt.

"No," she said, as she kneeled on the bed. "Let me."

He let his hands drop to his sides as she reached up to undo his buttons. With every button she opened, she deposited a kiss on his newly exposed skin. His entire body was rigid as he tried to stop himself from becoming an animal, and simply throw her down and push inside her. His dick ached for release but he tried to think of something else as she slowly removed his shirt. She wanted to take off his shirt—so he would let her take off his shirt, even if it meant he had to bite the inside of his mouth until he bled, to stop from touching her.

As soon as she had his shirt off, it was her turn to lean down and suck on one of his tiny nipples, and he almost came, right then and there.

"*Fuck,*" he groaned, and then he pushed her down gently on her back.

He crawled over her, his naked chest pushed up against her luscious breasts, skin-to-skin for the first time. She was shaking, and her eyes looked almost feral with lust, and he realized that she needed some release now in order to enjoy all that he planned to do with her later. So, he sat up and pulled the sweatpants and her panties down and off her in one fell swoop. The vision of her, completely naked on his bed, her dark skin flushed and nipples hard from his ministrations, would forever be burned into his brain.

"You are so sexy," he murmured, and she smiled lovingly at him.

"Vlad," she sighed as he quickly kissed his way down her body.

When he kissed down her hips to her knees, he stopped. He looked up at her as he put both of his hands on her thighs and spread her legs. Her head was thrashing around on his pillow when her scent hit his nose. He almost buckled then, and his dick pulsed in his pants once, twice, and then stopped when he bit on the inside of his mouth as hard as he was able. She smelled like citrus and honey, and his mouth actually watered, he wanted to taste her so much.

He ran his index finger down the middle of her pussy, reveling in how wet she was. She bucked her hips up and he used his other hand to hold her down gently.

"Baby, it's okay," he told her, even though he wasn't sure that she could hear him at that point.

Her nipples were hard, and her pussy was pink and swollen—she was close.

"*Please*," she moaned, and he leaned down and licked up her entire opening, from her hot cove to her clit, in one long stroke.

His balls tightened up close to his body, and he prayed he wouldn't come yet. He licked her again, this time spreading her lower lips with his fingers. She tasted like the sweetest ambrosia in the world, and he knew then that she could crush his heart if she wished. He swallowed all of her sweet juice while she moved around the bed, unable to stay still. Finally, when he knew she couldn't take much more, he whispered, "Here you go, sweetheart," and pushed two fingers inside her.

She screamed, he sucked her hard clit into his mouth and pumped his hand, and she shattered. Her walls pulsed against his fingers over and over again, and he gently licked her, but avoided the ultra-sensitive clit, while she shuddered and thrashed.

Eventually, she lay still on the bed, her skin more flushed with pink than before. But when he crawled up her body, her face was clear and her eyes were focused on him.

"I can't move. That was incredible," she rasped, and he laughed softly.

He kissed her gently, his tongue sharing how she tasted with her. "*Delicious*," he said, after her questioning glance, and she smiled.

"It's your turn," she said a moment later, as they held each other.

"No, you don't have to do that."

"I want to."

"I want to make love to you," he said bluntly, his cock so hard and his balls so tight, that talking was difficult.

She smiled knowingly. "Come here," she said, and he gave up then. Was he really going to deny himself the pleasure of Thania's mouth surrounding his dick?

He lay down since he almost felt faint at that point, and she kneeled next to him on the bed.

"This won't take very long," he warned her, a little embarrassed at how quickly he knew he was going to come.

"That's alright," she assured him in a sexy whisper. "We'll be able to make love longer this way."

He smiled and then he groaned as he watched her take the tip of his length into her mouth, pulling back on his foreskin. She swirled her tongue around, and he gripped the sheets tightly.

"*Thania*," he moaned, when she licked him from tip to stem, and then pushed her mouth down his length.

She wasn't able to get his entire length in her mouth, but that didn't matter, because to Vlad, her soft, hot tongue, and her tight, warm mouth, felt better than having sex with most of his former partners. So, when she bobbed her head up and down on him, he exploded inside her mouth in no time at all. His climax was a sweet, piercing agony, followed by the most exquisite release of is life. When it was over, he felt relaxed but more alive than ever.

"Thank you," he told her, and she smiled as she lay down beside him and snuggled in. He put his arm around her and, with her head on his shoulder, they both fell asleep.

* * *

He woke up sometime in the night to Thania kissing his neck, and rubbing her hands along his chest. In moments, he was rock hard again.

"Thania," he whispered into the darkness of the bedroom.

"Mmmm," she replied, her mouth otherwise occupied with his nipples. She moved up and straddled him, and he realized her intentions.

"No, not like that," he said, as he wrapped his arms around her and flipped them both over, so that he was on top.

"Why?" she whispered, sounding bewildered.

"Because," he replied, as he gently pushed her hair off her forehead, "I want the memory of looking down into your eyes as we made love."

He saw her smile, and he leaned down to kiss her, this time just as sensuous as the first. He reached over to his nightstand and quickly put on a condom.

"Are you ready for me?" he whispered as she spread her legs, and he nudged her entrance with his cock.

"I'm not sure," she replied honestly, and he laughed softly.

"Well, too bad, then," he said with a smile, and then she pulled his head down for another kiss.

After a few seconds, he pulled away so he could watch her face as he pushed his way into her. She was wet again, and his dick throbbed to be inside her. Her pussy felt like a sucking vise against his cock, and they both moaned as he slid all the way in on one push. They both breathed deeply as her body adjusted to him. He was shaking already with the need to thrust, but he waited.

"You are incredible, Thania," he said, and she reached up and touched his face so gently that something inside him broke a little.

This woman has changed me.

He kissed her again as he slowly moved inside her, his body reveling in what felt like the most exquisite pleasure of his life. No one else would ever compare to her, he was sure of that now. They moved together slowly at first, gently, as if love was in the room with them. But soon, lust moved in, and they were both pushing and pulling, harder and harder. She felt so good underneath him that he started to pump into her, searching for the pinnacle that he knew was within reach.

But he wanted her to find release first, so he leaned down and sucked her nipple into his mouth, making love to her breasts while she moaned underneath him.

He pulled up and thrust his tongue in her mouth, as he moved one hand down between their bodies to her clit. It was hard, and he pushed the hood aside gently, as he continued to thrust his cock into her.

"*Vlad*," she groaned against his lips, and he knew he couldn't hold out much longer.

She felt too good. So he pushed hard on her clit and she came, her tight tunnel milking his dick to the point of pain. Once her body had stopped quivering, she grabbed his head with both hands and kissed him hard. She lifted her knees and he placed his hands behind them, pushing them down toward the mattress so that she was open as wide as possible.

He rammed into her then, their bodies making the music first heard millions of years ago. She was moaning and he was sweating, and he knew he would never be the same again after this night with her. But he wanted this, he wanted her, and that was his last thought, before he came so hard that he was momentarily blinded by the explosions rocketing throughout his body.

Chapter 7

Thania

Thania woke up in Vlad's arms, the sun shining through his windows onto her face. From the angle of the rays, she could tell it was still quite early, probably just after dawn.

Her body ached in that delicious just-had-amazing-sex way, and she sighed. It was the best night of her life, if she was honest with herself, but she hated to admit it. Admitting it meant that she might feel hurt when he didn't call or ask her out again. And he had made it clear last night that this was a one-time deal.

"…once the stores are stable, I'll be heading back to Russia."

"I want the memory of looking down into your eyes as we made love."

She knew before they slept together that this was a one-off for him. She hadn't cared then, and had decided to sleep with him anyway, so there was no point in wanting something she could not have. She was a practical woman with a phenomenal career ahead of her, and she did not have time to worry about Vlad, or any other man for that matter.

You are running away before he can.

She looked at him as he slept beside her, his face and body so beautiful to her that she felt tears well up. She pushed them back down, and snuggled into his arms for just one more minute. In his sleep, Vlad pulled her closer against him, and kissed her temple.

Just be glad that you had this time with him. You'll be fine.

She decided to creep out of bed and leave before he woke up. It was cowardly, she could admit that too, but it seemed like a better alternative to a conversation that ended with "see you never." She moved out from under his arm slowly, praying he wouldn't wake up. After a full five minutes, she tried to slide off the bed gracefully, but flopped onto the floor and landed on all fours, frozen. She waited to hear if he had woken up, but he didn't move at all.

This is really dignified.

She crawled across the plush carpet and grabbed the sweatpants, pulling them on. She couldn't find her panties after a ten second search, so she gave up on them. She couldn't remember where the t-shirt was until she thought really hard. Vlad had removed it in the hallway last night, so with her face flushed at the memory of The Hallway Incident, she crawled out there and retrieved the shirt.

She felt almost victorious as she slowly stood up after putting on the t-shirt. She really wanted to get out of there before he woke up and they had a super awkward encounter. She was a big girl, and she could accept last night for what it was—two adults simply enjoying themselves.

She watched Vlad from the doorway for a few moments, trying to convince herself that she wasn't memorizing how he looked as he slept. She had finally turned to leave, her chest aching, when she spotted her dress hanging in Vlad's closet next to his bed.

Cursing inwardly, she dropped down to all fours again and crawled over the entire expanse of his enormous bedroom to the closet. She stood up slowly, attempting to make as little noise as possible, and removed the ruined gown from the hanger. Ruefully, she rolled it up and tucked it under one arm before dropping to the floor once again. And right there, in her line of sight, were her custom made heels.

Sounding like a truck driver inside her own head, she leaned forward and grabbed the shoes. Having convinced herself that the only chance for a dignified retreat was to crawl, she put the straps of the shoes into her mouth, tucked the dress under her arm again, and made much slower progress toward the bedroom door.

This is not a good look.

Annoyed at her inner commentary, she stood up immediately when she reached the door for the second time. She glanced back at Vlad for only a minute this time, figuring she had already pushed her luck enough, before she turned and jogged lightly down the hallway.

She found her clutch in the living room and pulled out her phone to call a taxi. Unbelievably, she was told it would take forty-five minutes for them to get to Vlad's home. Knowing that staying there was not an option, she tiptoed to the foyer, and opened the fifteen foot arched solid mahogany doors with as little noise as possible.

She made it, she thought after she shut the enormous doors behind her. She lightly jogged down the front steps and stepped onto the driveway.

Damn, it was a pebbled forecourt, something she hadn't remembered from last night. But she had been wearing heels last night, and had been so shocked by the size of Vlad's home, that the driveway could have been on fire for all she would have noticed.

Get on with it. Don't be such a sissy. You did not do all that crawling just to get caught now.

So she started to walk down the driveway, hopping from one bare foot to the other, as the pebbles hurt her feet. She considered putting her high heels back on, but figured she was already enough of a hot mess— shimmery, four-inch silver sandals did not need to be added to the mix. It was bad enough that she had stolen his clothes. She figured he would consider it a small price to pay in exchange for her having left before he woke up, thereby alleviating him from the 'morning after' talk.

I am quite the benevolent soul.

Wondering what, exactly, she had done to piss off Karma, she continued to trudge down the driveway, the stones cutting into her delicate feet. Even so, she felt freedom looming in front of her. She was almost to the street, where she could just find a shady patch of grass to sit on while she waited for the taxi.

Then she turned the last corner and saw it—Vlad's closed gate—something else she apparently had not noticed last night.

* * *

It stood there before her like the Berlin Wall. On one side was an embarrassment of riches (emphasis on 'embarrassment'), and on the other side was freedom.

She knew that was not exactly the history of the Berlin Wall, but she was out of time to consider other metaphors. She needed to be on the other side of that obstacle.

Slowly, she walked up to the huge gate (why was everything so gigantic here?), and stared at the electronic keypad that allowed access to and from the house.

Not the 'house'. The mansion. The estate. The castle. Whatever.

She was irritated now, which was much more preferable to the fear of being discovered. She figured there was no way Vlad would see her out here so far

from the house. *The mansion, the estate, the castle,*
whatever.

She had absolutely no idea what the code could be,
and there was no way she was going to try some
combinations and hope she figured it out. With her
awful luck this morning, the police would come after
the third wrong code. So, she took the only remotely
feasible option at that point.

I'm going to climb it.

Never mind that the gate was solid wood, with
barely any places for footholds or handholds. And
never mind that the last thing she had climbed was a
tree over twenty years ago—she could do this. Well,

there was the rock wall at the gym—she'd climbed that, right?

You never climbed that. You walked up to it, looked up to the top, told your personal trainer to shove off, and threw your helmet in the bin.

Ignoring all detractors, even the one inside her head, she tossed her clutch up and over the gate. Except she didn't quite make it, and the clutch hit the gate, opened up, and fell with all of its contents raining down upon her. She heard the crash of her cell phone on the pebbles, and her lipstick hit her on top of her head. She sighed and tried again—there was no way that she could climb the gate while holding all of her stuff. She tossed the cellphone again, and it made it to the other side, which she considered a victory.

Great, now you have a broken cellphone on the opposite side of the wall. Go you.

Flinging her wallet, clutch, and lipstick with much more gusto, she got them each over on the first try. Or second, but why be technical? She was equally as successful with each of the shoes and the dress. Well, one of the shoes was stuck in a tree on the other side, but so what? It was on the other side.

Feeling the adrenaline flow through her at the thought of imminent freedom, she figured she needed to get herself over the gate too, since it was probably pretty close to forty-five minutes at that point, and all she needed now was a taxi continuously honking and waking up Vlad, while she was still stuck on this side of the gate.

She placed one bloodied foot on the bottom "rung" of the gate, and was just about to step up, when she noticed a bright pink cylindrical shape on 'her' side of the gate. Sighing, she got down. It was her never-leave-home-without-it emergency tampon. It must have fallen out of her clutch, too. She could just imagine Vlad finding that—her humiliation would be complete.

Having no pockets, no bra, and no panties to stuff the tampon in, she put it in her mouth like she was a dog holding a stick. It would occur to her later that she should have tossed it over the gate like the other items, and her only excuse would be that she had been trying to think without coffee. Really, coffee had magical qualities. It made her funnier, nicer, and definitely smarter.

So she tried again, this time with the tampon firmly clenched in her mouth. She put her foot on the little ledge she called a rung, and pulled herself up about four inches.

At this rate, you'll be over by this time next week. Vlad will never notice.

Determined to get over the damned gate come hell or high water, she kept going. The only other option was to head back to the house. *Mansion, estate, castle, whatever.* She'd have to wake Vlad up, and explain to him her misadventures, and at that point, climbing the metaphorical Berlin Wall seemed preferable.

"Going somewhere?"

* * *

She turned around slowly while she still clung to the gate, four inches above the ground.

There stood Vlad, all handsome and debonair, with a gigantic grin on his face.

"Erhmm," was the sound that came out of her mouth before she remembered the bright pink tampon, spit it out, and tried again. "Actually, yes," she said with conviction.

Die on the hill, girl. Die on the hill.

"Can I help you in some way?" he said, as he walked right up to her and lifted her off the gate.

"Hey!"

"It's okay, Thania. If you really want to leave, I will have my driver take you home. There was no need for you to go through all of…this," he said as he gestured

to the pebbled driveway and the bright pink tampon.
He placed her gently on the ground, and she
immediately flinched in pain.

"What's wrong?" he exclaimed.

"Nothing," she mumbled, moving from one foot to
the other. "It's just that my feet…"

"Let me see," he demanded, and she decided that
she did not like his tone.

"No."

"What? Why?" he demanded again. "I *can* help you,
you know," he continued as he smiled gently at her.

Maybe you should die on another hill. Some other day.

"Okay," she said softly, and he immediately picked her up again and then sat down with her on his lap.

"Let me see."

She turned one foot over, and he made a tsk-tsking sound in the back of his throat. She tried to pull her foot away but he wouldn't let her.

"Stop," he said, and she crossed her arms. "This is bad, Thania. What were you thinking?"

She looked at him as he gently held her foot in his hand, and wondered the same thing.

"I wanted to leave," she said simply, as if her behavior had been perfectly normal.

"Okay. Why didn't you just wake me up? I would have driven you myself, or had my driver take you if you preferred." He made it all sound so reasonable, as if she hadn't had to worry about an awkward conversation.

I think it's safe to say at this point that we did not avoid the awkward conversation.

"I don't know. I just wanted to leave," she said again, while she tried not to feel his body against hers, and tried not to notice that his chest was bare and so, so sexy in the early sunlight.

"Let's go in the house," he suggested. "Stay with me."

Her heart lurched when she heard that, but she quickly convinced herself that it wasn't what he meant —it must've been just a language issue.

Ignoring her confusion, Vlad picked her up and carried her down the driveway, as if she weighed nothing.

Was there anything this man couldn't do, she wondered. He'd taken a few steps back to the house when she told him to stop.

"I need my stuff," she said to the front of his naked neck.

"What stuff?" he asked as he looked around. "Do you mean that bright pink thing?"

"No! I mean my other stuff. You know, my clutch and my dress and my shoes…"

"Well, where are they?" He turned around in circles while he looked for her stuff, and soon she was dizzy.

She told him to stop again. "It's on the other side of the Berlin Wall."

"Excuse me?"

"Your gate! It's like the Berlin Wall! Impossible to climb!"

He still held her, but she could tell he was trying very hard not to laugh. *Jerk*, she thought unkindly.

"The Berlin Wall, huh?" he said, and he burst out with laughter, the sound so rich and satisfying, that she couldn't help smiling herself.

"How did you get your stuff over the Berlin Wall?" he asked, still laughing.

"I threw it," she replied and he laughed again.

He walked over to the electronic key pad, punched in a short code, and she felt like she was watching the parting of the Red Sea.

"Well, that was easy," she said dryly.

He giggled—actually giggled—as he carried her through the gate to find her stuff. He walked over to the grass and put her down gently, and then he went all around to gather up her things.

"Did the Berlin Wall do this?" he asked, as he held up her shattered cellphone.

"Sort of," she replied, and he hid a smile.

"It seems you have somehow misplaced a shoe," he said seriously, after depositing the rest of her things in her lap.

"It's up in the tree," she mumbled.

"Pardon?"

"I *said*, It's. Up. In. The. Tree."

He looked up to where she pointed, saw her sparkly high heel, and promptly went over to climb the tree and retrieve her shoe.

"Thank you," she said stiffly as he placed it in her lap with her other things.

"What were you trying to avoid?" he asked her seriously, after some tense silence.

"An awkward conversation," she replied, and then she burst out laughing, and he followed suit. She laughed until her sides ached, and then she felt so much better about the entire thing.

"Come on, Berlin frau," he said as he swung her up into his arms again. "Let's take care of you."

* * *

And he did take care of her. He sat her down in one
of his massive kitchen chairs, and dragged out a First
Aid kit. She insisted she could do it herself, but he
wouldn't let her.

"What if you stab yourself with these incredibly
sharp scissors?" he said as he held up a tiny pair of
scissors, maybe two inches long, with a rounded, safety
tip.

"Very funny."

But he'd been very sweet, and cleaned out every one of the cuts on her feet before putting on some antibiotic ointment and wrapping them like she'd broken her ankles.

"Isn't this a bit much?"

"I've realized that with you, I can never be too careful."

She rolled her eyes at him, and then he made them breakfast. She had been completely relaxed by then, as she ate a delicious omelet and drank some superb coffee.

"This was so good, thank you," she said sincerely, as she sat back in her seat.

"I'm glad you think so. And you're welcome," he replied. Suddenly, the awkwardness was there again, front and center.

"I had such a nice time with you last night," he said after about a minute of silence.

A nice time?

"Yes, I did, too. I really enjoyed the gala, thank you for inviting me."

He looked closely at her then, as if trying to figure her out.

"You didn't have to sneak out like that this morning, Thania."

"Oh, I know," she said breezily, determined not to show how much she already cared for him. "I just have so much to do today. I've got my new fashion show coming up soon, I think I mentioned that."

"Yes, you did," he replied slowly, still searching her face.

She felt herself start to blush, and he finally looked away.

"Can you arrange for your driver to take me home, please? I really have a lot to do today," she repeated, her feelings way too close to the surface for her liking. She needed to get out of there.

"Yes, of course."

He stood up slowly and looked down at her for a few seconds without saying anything. Then, he walked over to a phone on the kitchen counter, pressed a button, and had a brief conversation with someone in Russian. After that, she went to the restroom and hung out in there for ten minutes, ostensibly cleaning up, but really she was killing time until the driver was ready. She dreaded saying goodbye to Vlad.

Don't think about it. At least he hasn't said he'll call you sometime.

He knocked on the bathroom door, jolting her into turning off the water that had been running the entire time she'd been inside. She opened the door, and Vlad stood there with a small bag filled with the items she'd tried to escape with. He handed it to her and she started to walk to the front door, as he followed slowly.

When she reached the big mahogany doors, she turned and kissed him on the cheek. He looked surprised, but before he could say anything she started down the steps toward the driver and the town car that waited for her. She turned and waved goodbye jauntily.

Don't say anything. Please, for the love of God, please don't let him say anything.

"I had a really nice time," he called out to her, but she didn't turn around. "I'll call you sometime!" he yelled just before the driver slammed the door.

She was heartbroken.

* * *

"He said he'd call me sometime," she said into her cellphone.

Both Asha and Daya groaned. She knew they would want an account of the gala, so she decided to get it over with on the ride home.

"You've got to be *kidding* me," Asha said, for once sounding animated. "Men are such assholes," she continued, and Thania heard Daya laugh.

"Vlad isn't an asshole," Thania said, and her friends were silent. "He's really not," she insisted as she wondered why she was bothering.

She wasn't going to see him again. At that thought, her chest constricted and she took a deep breath to keep from crying.

"He was very clear that he does not want a relationship," she continued. "I knew what I was getting into when I slept with him."

"You *slept* with him?" Daya practically screeched into her ear, and Thania heard Asha's familiar sigh.

"What, you thought she spent the night so they could play Jenga?" Asha said.

"Yes, I did," Thania said, feeling defensive. "And it was amazing," she added, and even she could hear the wistful tone of her voice.

"Was he uncircumcised?" Daya asked unceremoniously. "I've heard most Russian guys are uncut."

"Stop this line of questioning, right now, Daya," Thania hissed into the phone.

"Oh, shit," Daya said, more somber now.

"She's in love with him," Asha announced.

"Yup," Daya immediately concurred.

"Wait a minute…" Thania tried to interject.

"Well, I can't really blame her," Daya said, as if she were only speaking to Asha. "He's handsome, rich, and he's got that good guy shtick going on."

"It's not a shtick," Thania protested, and then it occurred to her that she should not care what her best friends said about Vlad. She didn't need to defend him, or proclaim his virtues. They'd had one night together. One fabulously memorable, sexy as hell night, but that was all it would ever be. "Don't worry," she interrupted her two friends as they continued to discuss her and Vlad as if she weren't on the phone. "I know the score," she continued. "It was one night of fun, and it's over. Now, I can concentrate on the fashion show."

"That's right, honey," Asha said, and the conversation moved on to her friends' lives.

Thania listened, and made all the appropriate comments at the appropriate times, but inside she was reliving last night with Vlad. She would not regret that she'd spent the night with him because it had been the most amazing night of her life. And she'd known before she had slept with him that he wasn't looking for anything more than one night.

So, even though she knew all of that, why was she still so sad?

Chapter 8

Vlad

Vlad played his night with Thania over in his mind as he listened to her voicemail tell him she was unavailable for the fifth time. It had been a week since their night together, and all he could do was think about her.

He didn't understand why she was avoiding him, because by now it was clear that she was doing just that. He had been so sure that she felt something for him, too. It was more than just sex, although frankly, for him, the sex had been life altering. Life altering,

meaning, he couldn't imagine touching another

woman besides Thania ever again.

Before the gala, he had been very interested in and

intrigued with Thania. After the gala, and the night

they had spent together, he was consumed with her.

She was all he thought about, night and day. He was

driving his friends crazy. He couldn't concentrate on

his work, and he was having trouble sleeping.

He hesitated to think of the L word, even to himself,

but that was because he had never told a woman,

outside of his family, that he loved them. It was a huge

deal to him to say the words, and he did not take it lightly.

Even so, he was pretty sure that he was in love with Thania. A friend had once told him that you know that you are in love when you feel physically ill at the thought that the other person didn't love you back. He said that's why it's called 'falling in love', because you feel unmoored and out of control, especially at the very beginning when you are unsure of the other person's feelings.

Well, he certainly felt unmoored and out of control, and he hated it. He was miserable.

"Just call her, already," Maks said from across the conference table, when it became apparent that Vlad was not paying attention once again.

"I did. I have," Vlad responded impatiently, not even trying to pretend that he didn't know to whom Maks was referring.

Vlad knew that his friends were sympathetic, but only up to a certain point. Neither of them had been in love, so they had no first-hand knowledge to share with him. In addition, they had never seen Vlad act like this before, and they had no idea what to say to him.

"Well, it's five o'clock in homeland," Maks said, as he pushed his chair back and headed for the built in bar.

"It's five o'clock *here*," Mick pointed out, and Maks laughed.

"So it is. That must mean something."

"Yes, it means pour me a drink," Vlad said darkly, and Maks soon complied. He placed a crystal glass in front of Vlad, and from Vlad's estimation, it was a double.

"Trying to tell me something?" he asked sardonically, after he had knocked back at least half of the drink.

"Yes. You need to contact her," Maks said again.

"*I have!*" Vlad roared, and then he smacked one fist down upon the table, causing all of the glasses to jump dangerously.

Neither of the other men had any outward reaction, but they did exchange glances with each other.

"Take it easy on the two-hundred year old crystal," Mick said mildly, and Vlad looked sheepish.

"I apologize for my behavior," he said, as he swirled the vodka around in his glass some more, before downing the rest of the contents.

"It's fine, Vlad," Maks insisted. "We just don't know what to say to help you. This is not exactly our area of expertise," he continued with a laugh, managing to coax a smile out of Vlad.

"Alright, let us look at this like we would a business situation," Mick said, and Vlad raised an eyebrow at him but remained silent. If his friends were willing to help him, he would take whatever he could get.

"If this was a business deal that you really wanted to land, what would you do?" Mick asked, already knowing the answer.

Maks smiled and brought the vodka bottle over to the conference table, and filled everyone's glasses again. This might be a long meeting.

"I would keep at it, going around whatever obstacle was in my path, until I had what I wanted," Vlad answered without looking up from his glass.

"Exactly!" exclaimed Maks, and Vlad looked over at him, not quite understanding the point yet.

"You need to track her down, remove all of the obstacles, and not stop until you get what you want," Maks explained.

"Thania's not a business deal, Maks," Vlad replied with a sigh.

"Of course, she isn't. But the same principles apply," Mick said. "You can't be the only one that felt something when you two were together—my guess is that she felt the same things. You said it yourself, you have amazing chemistry…"

"Be careful," Vlad warned, his voice curt.

He had made the 'chemistry' comment earlier in the week, and his friends had been trying to get him to explain exactly what he meant ever since. But he would never speak about Thania that way, and it pissed him off that they thought he would. As the week wore on though, and his friends could see that he wasn't changing his mind about Thania, they had started to take the whole situation a lot more seriously.

"I'm not asking you for details, don't worry," Mick said. "I got the message when you practically punched me earlier in the week when I told you I liked the dress she wore to the gala," he continued, with a pointed look at Vlad.

"I'm sorry," Vlad replied, flushing under Mick's gaze.

"It's alright, my friend. I just don't know what it is like to want to protect a woman so much. But to get to the point—if this were a business deal that you absolutely wanted to close, you would let nothing stand in your way to get it."

"I can't exactly kidnap her and force her to spend time with me," Vlad responded, taking another sip of his vodka.

"No, but you can stop calling her phone, only to get her voicemail twenty damn times a day," Maks interjected.

"It's not twenty times a day…" Vlad protested weakly.

"It doesn't matter," Mick interrupted them both. "You need time with her, and what you're doing right now is not working. Right?" At Vlad's curt nod, Mick continued, "She has a new fashion show in a few days, right? She must be incredibly busy with that. I suggest that you get a ticket to the show and surprise her there. The hard work will be over by then, and she might be more receptive to you." Mick finished and pushed back from the table to stand up.

Vlad knew from experience when Mick was done discussing a subject, and that time had just come and gone.

"I think that sounds like a good plan. A good first start, if you will," Maks said, taking over where Mick had left off.

"Maybe. I don't want to bother her at her business, though."

"Do you even *hear* yourself?" Maks asked. "These are not the words that my friend Vladislav Sakharov would normally say. You need to get into business mode. Then go out and get what you want."

"Okay. I'll try it," Vlad said. He had nothing to lose by attempting to see her.

Except your pride.

He was past the point of caring about his pride, however. That was something else he'd learned about love this week.

* * *

Two days later, Vlad was feeling more in control. He had managed to get a ticket to Thania's fashion show the next day, and he had taken some other steps in the hopes of showing her that she was extremely important to him.

His assistant, Karen, buzzed him on the intercom.

"Yes, Karen?"

"The event organizer you wanted to speak to is on Line One. Also, I've arranged for the flowers you requested to be delivered this afternoon. The shop would like to know what you want the card to say."

Vlad dictated a quick message out to Karen. His plans were coming along nicely. He picked up Line One.

"Elsa, it's Vladislav here. How are the plans we have discussed coming along?"

Chapter 9

Thania

It was the day of Thania's second fashion show, and in many ways she felt as if this one was more important than the first. Critics would be looking for any flaw so that they could point out that she was a one hit wonder, and no one should believe the hype.

If that happened, all of her progress would halt, and most likely, her business would go under. That was why she had spent almost every minute of the last week in the studio where the fashion show would take place. She needed to supervise and oversee every single detail, so she would know that everything was at its absolute best.

She had hand picked every model, and every outfit. She had altered the designs herself, by hand, because she didn't trust anyone else to make sure the model's clothes fit perfectly. The designs had to look like they were made for each individual model's body, and she had worked to the point of exhaustion to make sure that happened.

Unfortunately, Vlad had been in her thoughts as well that week. That morning, she had stepped out of the shower, having thought about her night with Vlad while she scrubbed away her exhaustion. She had only had about three hours of sleep, and was even a bit hung over, since she had become sentimental last night and bought a bottle of the wine that she and Vlad had enjoyed together.

But of more concern to her than being hung over, today of all days, was that thoughts of Vlad were prominent in her mind. As she straightened her hair with a flat-iron, she closed her eyes and felt his hands on her breasts, heard him whisper her name, saw his face above her in the dark as he came. Damn it, she thought, as she turned off her Chi hair straightener, and walked into her bedroom to get dressed for the day. Okay, the sex had been amazing, but it was time to move on. Actually, it had been time to move on a week ago. But her body and her mind did not want to cooperate.

And Vlad wasn't helping either. He had called her a few times earlier in the week, but when she didn't answer, he had stopped. She had been relieved and incredibly sad at the same time. She missed him, however hard that was for her to believe, since they had only spent one night together.

She was stunned yesterday when he had sent another beautiful vase of flowers to her apartment. They were waiting on the mat outside of her apartment when she got home, and she stopped dead when she spotted them.

I can't do this.

It hurt so much to pretend to the world that she cared nothing for Vlad. But her pride would not allow her to do otherwise. So when she saw the flowers, any forward movement she had made to get over him was blown out of the water.

Who are you kidding? You still feel the exact same way about him.

Warily, she picked up the enormous vase and opened up her apartment. She set the flowers on the same table as last time, and stared at it like it was a

Venus flytrap. They were orchids this time, the same

type he had given her the night of the gala, and there

was another note sticking out of the middle, in the

same stationery that Vlad had used before. She circled

the table for a few minutes before she finally snatched

the note and tore it open:

Dearest Thania,

I wish you the best of luck

tomorrow with your fashion show.

You have worked so hard and you

deserve every success.

I know we are both extremely busy, but I see no reason why we cannot remain in contact, and check in with each other periodically. Our night together was special to me, and I hope it was to you as well.

Here is my personal cell phone number. Feel free to call me at anytime.

Warmest Regards,

~Vlad~

She didn't know what to make of his note, and she still didn't a day later. But today, the fashion show had to come first over everyone and everything else, so she would tuck Vlad away into a corner of her mind, to explore when she was able.

* * *

She arrived at the studio where the fashion show was being held, later than she planned. She had originally thought she would arrive just four hours before the show began, since she would have been there almost the entire previous night. But with her small hangover, and her constant thoughts about Vlad, she had gotten to the studio just three hours before the start of the show.

The models, makeup artists, and hair stylists were all due to arrive four hours before the start, so she had her first sense of foreboding when she pulled into the parking lot and the only other cars she saw belonged to Asha and Daya. She rushed into the studio, only to be greeted by absolute silence in the cavernous space, and the nervous faces of her two best friends.

"What's going on? Where is everyone?" Her heart was racing, and not in an excited, oh wow the roller coaster has a ninety foot drop, kind of way. More like in the not so fun, I am going to throw up on the teacups ride, kind of way.

"We don't know, Thania," Daya said with both of her hands up in front of her like she was surrendering to the police.

Thania would have laughed if she didn't want to cry.

"I don't understand," she said, refusing at the moment, to let her panic consume her. She needed facts. "This place should be teeming with thirty models, ten makeup artists, ten hair stylists. Never mind my wardrobe people—where are they?"

"Oh, we saw them!" Asha exclaimed, seemingly happy to be able to provide some positive news. "The wardrobe people went on a coffee run, and they'll be right back," she finished.

Despite the slightly scary thought of coffee near any of her new designs, Thania felt slightly better.

"Well, Daya," she said, "think you can wear all thirty designs?" Thania was only half kidding, the panic she had held at bay earlier slamming into her now with the force of a tsunami.

Her hands tingled, her feet were numb, and the center of her chest hurt so much that she could not take a deep breath. Luckily, Asha and Daya recognized the signs because Thania could no longer speak.

"Okay, honey," Asha said, as she and Daya physically guided Thania outside for some fresh air.

Once outdoors, it took a few minutes for Thania to be able to take deep enough breaths that the feeling came back in her extremities.

This is going just like I was afraid it would. 'Former Top Designer Uses One Model in her Fashion Show: Is She Cheap or just Stupid?'

She laughed, because otherwise she would have cried, as Asha and Daya got on their phones, each calling the models after Thania had pulled the list out of her bag. Up to that point, not a single one of them had answered.

"I'm sorry, love," Daya said, as she shook her head to the question of whether she had been able to reach anyone.

Her eyes looked so sad that Thania felt tears begin to well up in her own, but she didn't have time for that luxury, so she quickly wiped under her eyes and moved on.

"What else can we do? Who else can we call?" Asha asked fifteen minutes later, after they had called all of the phone numbers they knew.

For some reason that she couldn't explain, Vlad and his note from the day before, popped into Thania's mind.

"I have Vlad's phone number. I could call him," Thania said to the group at large, which now consisted of her two best friends, her two wardrobe people, and surprisingly, the makeup artist she had met at the photo shoot, Len.

"You have sugar's phone number?" Len asked, referring of course, to the fact that Vlad's last name translated to 'sugar' in Russian.

Every eye was on Thania.

"Yes," she said firmly, as she forced back any romantic thoughts of Vlad. There was absolutely no time for that now. There was an expectant silence after her one word answer.

"Well?" Len demanded, his irritation with her plain on his face. "What are you waiting for? The show to actually start with only one model?" he finished, as she happened to notice that his eggplant colored shirt matched very nicely with the lavender stripe he had put in his hair since the last time she had seen him.

"Yeah, Thania! Call Vlad, already!" Daya said emphatically, a look of panic in her own eyes by that time.

Thania knew that Daya did not want to be the only model available—this fashion show meant almost as much to Daya's career as it did to Thania's.

"What am I going to say to him?" Thania asked the group at large.

Again, silence.

"Ask him to help you," Asha said, speaking for the first time in a while.

"But, how can he help me? He runs a jewelry business," Thania said to her as sweat started to bead on her brow. She *really* did not want to call Vlad and ask him for help with *anything*, but she was getting past the point of desperation.

"Yes, he's in the jewelry business, Thania," Asha responded as if she spoke to a wounded animal. "That means that he most likely uses models himself for the jewelry ad campaigns. And at the very least, he knows other people in a similar business that might be able to help," she continued, as everyone watched her take charge of Thania by helping her see through her fear.

Thania knew it was obvious to everyone at that point, that Asha was her true friend, and that they had known each other forever.

"Go ahead, honey," Asha said to her, as she gently rubbed Thania's arms. "It can't hurt to call him."

So she did.

* * *

"Vlad, it's Thania," she said, when he answered his cellphone on the first ring.

"Hello," he said slowly in his gritty voice, and Thania flushed as she realized that he was not expecting her to call him.

And he probably doesn't want you to.

Forging ahead, because she had no choice, she said, "I am so sorry to bother you, Vlad. I'm in a bit of a bind, otherwise I would never have called you."

His silence was deafening to her, and she felt nauseated and needed to sit down.

"Today is the day of my fashion show," she started to explain, her heart actually aching as she spoke.

"Yes," he replied.

"Well, none of my models have shown up, and the show is supposed to begin in two hours! I don't know what is going on, and we've called all of them, and no one has answered. Daya is the only model here, and there is no way she can wear all of the clothes. How unprofessional would that look? And the press is starting to arrive, and I'm freaking out…"

"It's alright, Thania," he interrupted her softly. "Just tell me what I can do."

Her aching heart broke just a little more at his kind tone.

"I know that we're not dating, but is there any way you can call around to some business associates and ask about their models, or even models that you work with yourself, and ask them to come to my fashion show immediately?"

She was hugely embarrassed to put him out like this, and her anxiety reached its zenith once more as he remained silent on the phone. She heard him breathing, so she knew she hadn't lost the connection, and the longer it took for him to speak, the harder her chest constricted.

"Vlad? I'm sorry to have asked you," she said, resigned to the fact that she had crossed that invisible line between friends and 'something more'. And she definitely was not 'something more' to Vlad.

"No, no, it's fine," he quickly responded. "Yes, of course I can help."

Hope blossomed within her, and some of the ache in her chest subsided—not the broken heart part, though.

"You just hang tight, Thania," he continued in his deep voice. "I'll see what I can do."

"Thank you so much, Vlad," Thania said, grateful beyond words.

"You're welcome," he replied, and she could have sworn his voice sounded almost sad.

* * *

An hour later, the models started to arrive at the studio. They all rushed in, looking frantic, and Thania could not believe what they told her.

"Very early this morning, my phone rang, and it was a woman saying that she was a model in your first show, and that you never paid her—or any of the models," one girl explained. "She told me not to answer any calls from you or your office today. She said you'd fooled everyone last time."

"Yeah, I got that same phone call, too!" another model said.

"Who would do that?" Daya asked Thania.

Honestly, Thania had no idea. It turned out that every single model, except for Daya, had received the same call that morning. It sounded like professional jealousy to Thania, something an immoral competitor would do in order to sabotage her career. But she could not imagine who could be so threatened by the beginning of her success, that they would go to such an extreme to ruin her business.

"How did you know to come here?" Asha asked the group of models, and one spoke up.

"I got a call from—and you're not going to *believe* this—but it was from *Vladislav Sakharov*!" she exclaimed, clearly impressed with him.

Thania was stunned, and then completely astonished when every model started to talk at the same time, to tell her that they too, had received calls from Vlad. Apparently, he had told them that there had been a misunderstanding, and that whoever called them that morning was just playing an evil prank. He had asked them all to head down to the studio immediately, and every one of them had agreed and hopped in their cars. It was Vlad Sakharov asking, after all!

"It was so amazing to hear his voice…" a model gushed, and Thania just stood there, not knowing what to say.

"Yes, yes, I'm sure it was the highlight of your life," Len interrupted the model in a dry voice. "Now, let's get you all to makeup and hair, girls!" he said as he herded every model, including Daya, toward the makeup and hair stylist's area. "Right now, y'all look a bit ragged around the edges, and I'm sure that our lovely boss is not going for a ratchet theme for her show." Len turned toward Thania as he walked away, and gave her a wink. Something sweet bloomed inside her as she looked after him.

No matter how badly the situation with Vlad ended up, I think I've made a true friend in Len.

She smiled after him, her first true smile of the morning. She still could not believe that Vlad had managed to save the day, and her fashion show would move forward, and be on time. It was wonderful of him to make such an effort, and she wondered why he had.

And who was behind canceling the models to begin with? That was just unbelievable, and it made her so angry that her blood practically boiled. But she did not have time to think about any of that now; the backstage area teemed with models and stylists, and she could hear the crowd as the seats began to fill up on the other side of the stage.

This is it. This is the real turning point in my career.

And she intended to enjoy every moment of it.

Chapter 10

Vlad

Vlad sat in the front row of Thania's fashion show an hour later, pride swelling in his chest at what she had accomplished. The show was magnificent, she was magnificent, and the entire thing went off without a hitch. No one in the audience would ever know that it almost did not happen at all.

He watched Thania take the final walk down the runway, holding the hand of her last model, who was wearing a different, but equally beautiful gown than the one Thania had worn to the gala. The crowd gave her and her models a standing ovation, and she had a huge smile on her face as she waved at everyone.

He noticed that her cheeks were flushed, and it brought him back to their one night together. His cock twitched and hardened, much as it had every single time he'd had a single thought about Thania since that night. Which meant he was basically in a perpetual state of arousal.

He still didn't understand why she had pulled away from him like she had. Even on the phone earlier, she had said 'I know we're not dating', and hearing that from her was like an axe to his chest. He had known, of course, that she wasn't interested in seeing him again, simply from her behavior, but to hear her say the words aloud had actually stunned him. He had needed a minute to respond after he'd heard that.

Of course, he knew who had attempted to sabotage Thania's fashion show—Irina. One of the models he'd called earlier in the day had mentioned that the female caller had an unusual accent, and immediately, he had become almost murderous with rage. But only on the inside, because he would do nothing to ruin Thania's day any more than it already had been.

But as soon as he was able, he was going to track Irina down. He would make sure that she understood that she was never to bother Thania again, or to attempt to interfere with her career. He was livid at what Irina had done, but for now, he just allowed his pride for Thania to wash over him.

* * *

A half an hour later, Thania sought him out in the thinning crowd. She looked so beautiful that his heart twisted. He wanted her so badly, and for the first time in his life, he was broken-hearted.

"Congratulations, Thania," he said with a smile, as he kissed her on the cheek. Her scent almost overwhelmed him, and he longed to pull her into his arms and kiss her.

Just take the hint and move on.

"The show was incredible," he told her, and the flush traveled down her neck into her cleavage, and he dug his nails into his hands to keep from touching her.

"Thank you," she replied, as she looked him in the eye for the first time. Immediately, the pull was there between them again, and he wondered how she didn't feel it like he did. "And thank you for everything you did to save it. It would never have happened if you hadn't stepped in. I still can't believe that you called every one of the models yourself! They were all quite star struck," she said with an amused smile.

"You needed help," he said, as if it were that simple.

Their eyes connected again and her smile faltered. Suddenly, he couldn't stop himself anymore.

"Why did you pull away from me, Thania?" he asked, almost unable to believe that he had brought up the topic. But, he needed some answers if he ever wished to move on from her.

"Pull away from you? What do you mean?" she replied, a genuinely perplexed look on her face.

"I mean, I called you several times after our night together, and you never contacted me back."

"I…I…I have been working very hard this week," she stammered, visibly upset.

"I know, and I'm sorry to have brought this up here. I don't want to upset you," he said gently.

"No, no. I'm just surprised, that's all," she said, as she searched his eyes.

He wondered what she was looking for. "Surprised about what?"

"Surprised that you would say that *I've* pulled away from *you*."

Now he was the one who was confused. "Now you need to tell me what *you* mean," he said, as he took a step closer to her. His heart beat picked up as hope filled him.

She paused for a long time, and just looked at him without answering.

"I thought you had made it very clear that night we were together, that you were not interested in anything beyond that," she finally said, her face aflame and her arms crossed in front of her.

Hope burst into full bloom for him then, and he put his hands on her shoulders and gently pulled her arms away from her chest. She looked up at him warily.

"No, Thania. No," he said as he looked down into her eyes. She still looked confused so he decided to be blunt. "I didn't just want you for that one night. I want you for *every single night*."

She smiled and took the final half step necessary in order to push their bodies together.

"Really?" she asked him.

"Yes. Every. Single. Night," he said, and she reached up to wrap her arms around his neck.

He clutched her tightly to him and kissed her, falling into her just like he had before. He was so happy that he felt weightless, as if a gigantic boulder had been lifted from his shoulders. He pulled back slightly from the kiss but didn't let her go.

"So, you want to be with me, too? Me and only me?" He figured they'd had enough misunderstandings between them, and some clarification might be a good idea.

She laughed softly and smiled at him again. "Yes, Vlad. I want to be with you, and only you," she whispered, and he leaned down and kissed her once more, lifting her off her feet and turning in a slow circle as they kissed.

"Well, isn't this...*cozy*."

* * *

He pulled away from the kiss and set Thania down as he turned toward Irina.

"You shouldn't be here," he said to Irina quietly as he linked his fingers with Thania beside him.

"No, *you* shouldn't be here," she replied loudly as she swayed slightly. "*None* of you should be here," she continued, and he felt Thania stiffen at his side.

He squeezed her fingers softly to reassure her.

"I knew it was you," he said, and Thania gasped and flung his hand away.

Surprised, he looked warily at her. But she wasn't angry with him. Thania walked up to Irina.

"*You're* the one that tried to sabotage my show?" she asked Irina in a deceptively casual voice.

"Thania, let me talk to her…" he started, but he trailed off when Thania lifted her hand in a 'stop' signal to him.

Okay, then.

"I want to know her answer," she said pleasantly, without looking away from Irina.

"Of course, it was me, you stupid bitch," Irina said, causing several people surrounding them to turn and stare.

"What have I done to be called such foul names?" Again, Thania was poised and quiet.

"You stole my boyfriend!" Irina yelled, and after that a crowd formed around them.

Some members of the press were taking pictures, and Vlad even saw one man openly videotaping the argument. But he didn't dare try to intercede again; it was clear that Thania wanted to handle it herself.

"I did no such thing. You and Vlad have been broken up for more than six months. I didn't even know him six months ago."

"That's a lie! We're still together," Irina insisted with less vehemence that time.

Thania looked back at him and raised her brow in question.

"No," he said loudly. "Irina and I are not together. We broke up six months ago, and she refuses to let go."

Irina looked as if she wanted to argue, but Thania started to speak.

"Listen up, Irina," Thania said very softly. "If you ever try to interfere with or sabotage my business again, I will have you arrested. You are extremely lucky that my event went off without a hitch today because I would have sued you for every damned cent you have. And let me be clear: your time with Vlad is over. It is done. He wants nothing to do with you, whether I am in his life or not. Having Vlad as your enemy seems like a really bad decision to me. Seems like you would be better off leaving him alone, rather than risk his wrath. You'll probably never be able to book another modeling gig if you don't stop this right now."

"That's not true," Irina whispered.

"Yes, it is," Thania insisted. "And one more thing—from one woman to another—get some help for your drinking problem. That sure as hell is not a good look. Oh, and please remember: if you ever call me a bitch again, I will break you."

Irina gasped in outrage as Thania turned away from her. Vlad looked on with astonished pride—Thania had handled Irina beautifully. She had never raised her voice, or called the other woman names. She had just told her how it was going to be from then on.

Look at her. That beautiful woman is mine.

Thania walked up to him and grabbed his hand. They turned to walk through the gathered crowd, much like they had at the gala. Vlad glanced back to make sure Irina hadn't moved, and she was still standing where Thania had left her, looking a little broken as everyone around her pretended she wasn't there.

Chapter 11

Thania

"So, that is the entire story about Irina," Vlad finished as they stood outside of the studio in the sunshine.

Thania leaned up and kissed him, thrilled that she now could do so whenever she wanted. He immediately pushed her up against the outside wall of the studio, gently cradling her so that her skin and her clothes only touched his arms. Soon, they were kissing like teenagers, not caring about the rest of the world.

"I'm so glad that we talked today and ironed out our misunderstandings," he said after pulling back slightly.

She ran her fingers through his thick hair and he hummed in appreciation.

"Yes, me too," she agreed emphatically and then kissed him again. She couldn't seem to keep her hands off him, and Vlad responded in kind.

I can't believe how happy I am. We're together! Hopefully, someday, he'll want a future with me like I do with him.

She was done pretending to everyone, but especially to herself, that she wasn't in love with him.

She was head over heels, madly in love with Vlad, and it felt incredible to be in his arms again.

"Will you come and spend some time alone with me?" Vlad asked, his eyes so green in the sunlight that they looked almost iridescent.

"Of course." It wasn't even a question that needed to be asked, as far as she was concerned. All she wanted to do was be alone with him.

They went back inside to gather her things, and shortly after, they had arrived at a posh hotel downtown. As Vlad handed his keys to the valet, she asked him what was going on.

"How come we didn't go to your house? Mansion, estate, castle, whatever."

He laughed and looked at her oddly before grabbing her up in his arms once more.

"My *house* is too far away. So, while you grabbed your stuff, I made a quick call to the hotel and reserved a suite for us. You don't like it?" He nuzzled her neck while he waited for her response.

Oh, he feels so good. I can't wait to be alone and in bed with him.

"Oh no, I like it," she answered, and he took her hand, grabbed a room key from the waiting concierge, and strode over to the elevator banks, gently pulling her along the entire way.

"Do I need to carry you again?" he asked with a smile, as they entered the elevator. He punched in the necessary code for the penthouse and the elevator started its ascent.

"Maybe," she said coyly, and he leaned his whole body against her as they kissed.

Thania was so ready to be naked with him that her body was shivering. Finally, the elevator doors opened directly into the suite, but Vlad didn't stop kissing her. Until she heard,

"Surprise!"

* * *

Vlad had planned a surprise party for Thania in the suite. It turned out, he had been planning it for days, as a way to show her how much he cared and wanted to be with her. Part of her was thrilled by his sweet gesture, and part of her was vastly disappointed that they weren't going to be alone anytime soon.

"I can't believe you got me all worked up like that in the elevator," she whispered to him just before greeting her friends and family.

"Later, my love," he responded with a wink, and her stomach flip flopped.

He had invited her parents and brother, which was so wonderful of him. She introduced them all to each other, and her mom and dad seemed to approve. He had also invited her girlfriends Daya and Asha, and his friends Maks and Mick. All of the models and makeup artists and hair stylists from the show were there, even Len.

"Hey, doll," Len said when she said hello. "Seems that sugar likes your honey," he continued in a sing-song voice, and she playfully swatted him.

"Shut up," she said, with no venom and a big smile.

"Never, doll," he replied.

She and Vlad spent the afternoon and early evening playing hosts, and while she was so appreciative of his thoughtful gesture, the longer she looked at him talking to another person across the room, the more she wanted him. By the time the last person had left, she was in quite a state.

"I had such a wonderful time," she said as she kissed his mouth immediately after the elevator doors closed on the last guest.

"Mmm, you're welcome," he said as he swung her up into his arms and walked purposefully toward the bedroom. He placed her next to the bed.

She felt adrenaline rush through her body as she watched him watching her, his eyes roaming slowly over her generous breasts, after she'd taken off her blouse. Vlad was already breathing heavy and his eyes were half-closed. He sank down on his knees in front of her and reached up to unzip her skirt so she could take it off. He then lifted her feet to remove her heels, and he threw them on the floor.

When he didn't stand up right away, she put her hands on his shoulders to balance herself. He looked up and put his hands on the back of her thighs above her knees, and very slowly leaned his face in toward her panties.

She was shocked by an almost overwhelming need for him—and then he rested his face at the top of her thighs and inhaled her scent gently. She closed her eyes and tilted her head back, the pleasure of that moment causing her legs to almost give out. She moaned as he cupped her ass and pulled her sex closer to his face, so that he could inhale again. The ache in her pussy was almost painful.

She breathed very hard as her hands grabbed his shirt and made fists on his shoulders. She felt him drag one hand from her behind to the front of her panties. He took his index finger and slipped it underneath the lace, dragging his finger down past her clit until he was gently rubbing the folds of her pussy.

Her legs started to shake, and he said, "Look at me."

She looked down and he dragged his finger back up to her hard clit and stared into her eyes as he rubbed twice. She came so hard that she got light-headed and her knees finally buckled. When she was able to think again, he had placed her on the bed.

"*Vlad*," she groaned, and all she cared about at that moment was being with him.

He was so strong and she felt so feminine, and she had never before felt more powerful.

"You are so beautiful," he told her softly as he pushed her hair off her forehead.

"And you are so, so handsome," she responded as she reached down and took his dick in her hands.

"*God, Thania,*" he managed, as she massaged his cock with skillful hands.

After only a few minutes, he grabbed her hand to stop her. His tongue was in her mouth as he used one hand to guide his tip to her entrance. Then he grabbed her face gently with both hands as they kept kissing, while he slid all the way inside her. They both moaned —the feeling as he filled her up completely, while his breath was her breath, and his body weight pushed hers down into the bed, was indescribable.

She could feel his heart beat against her chest as she kissed him. His heart started beating even faster as he kissed her back—lush, sexual kisses that she knew would leave their mark on them both.

He pushed even further into the bed as he started thrusting in and out in a steady rhythm, and she came quickly and splendidly. When she did, he sped up as her muscles squeezed his cock, and he placed a hand behind one of her thighs, to open her further for his thrusts. He pumped over and over, harder and harder into her. The sounds and smells of sex surrounded them.

"I missed you so much," he managed to say.

"I missed you too, Vlad," she whispered in reply.

He put his face next to hers, their cheeks touching as he gripped her gently, and soon she was falling over the cliff with him. He collapsed on top of her, and she didn't want him to move, and he didn't seem able to, anyway. They lay that way for a while, his hand on the back of her head, his face next to hers, his body completely covering her like a blanket.

She moved her hands around his back, gently holding him. He moved his fingers to lightly rub the back of her neck.

"Thania, I love you," he said, as his heart started to slow against hers.

She thrilled at his words. "Oh, Vlad, I love you, too."

Chapter 12

Vlad

"Wake up, sleepy head," he said, hoping that Thania was a morning person.

After their last 'morning-after', he wasn't so sure. He held a steaming cup of coffee in his hand—black, no sugar—just the way she liked it, as he remembered that she was a lot more civil once she'd drank a cup on the 'Berlin Wall Day'.

She groaned after he gently shook her, and he braced himself.

"Hi, love," he said as she opened her eyes.

She blinked several times, and then sat up, but said nothing. He handed her the coffee and stood back, watching as she drank the entire cup in almost one gulp.

That was impressive.

"Another?" he asked, holding his hand out for the cup.

She gave it back to him, again without speaking. He watched her guzzle a second cup, and then, finally, she smiled at him.

"Good morning, my love," she said in her sweet voice, and he was so happy he thought his heart might explode in his chest.

"So, it takes two cups, huh?"

She lightly swatted his arm as she laughed.

"I have a surprise for you," he said, when he was sure the danger period was over.

"A surprise? *Another* one?" she asked, as she sat back against the pillows, looking to him like a goddess.

"Yes, another one."

"Well, what is it?"

"I can't tell you."

"What do you mean, you can't tell me? Remember, we got into trouble because we didn't explain things to each other before, Vlad."

She had a point, but he really wanted this to be a surprise.

"Nope, not telling. Can you get dressed, though? We leave in thirty minutes."

"Thirty minutes? Are you crazy? Do you know how long it takes a woman to 'get ready'?" She scowled at him.

"I know, my love. But I promise, you won't need to bring anything other than yourself. And I promise it will be worth it."

She looked like she didn't believe him.

"Do you trust me?" he asked.

"Of course."

"Then, get dressed, love."

* * *

————

THANIA

Seven hours later, she realized that trusting him had been a fabulous idea. He had driven her to a private landing strip right outside of the city, where they had boarded a private plane. His private plane. She still couldn't believe it. She had known that he was rich, of course, but she had not known the extent of his wealth.

Apparently, there were many levels of 'rich'. Vlad's seemed to be somewhere in the 'filthy' level.

He still refused to tell her where they were going, even once the flight took off. She knew they were headed south, because, well, the plane was headed south. But, beyond that, she had no idea. The farther south they went, the happier she became about the surprise. She began to envision a Caribbean island in her near future.

And she was correct. They landed on a tiny island in the Caribbean Sea that had no name. Vlad owned it, naturally, so she had upped his level of rich to 'obscene'.

They were greeted by some of Vlad's island staff that lived there year round. The island was absolutely stunning, with its pure white sand, aqua colored water, and tropical foliage. They were staying at Vlad's house on the island. And this time, it actually was a 'house'. Well, it was his house on his private island, but still. She decided not to quibble over the details.

The house was more like a very large version of a cottage. It had a beautiful, wide-planked wooden porch surrounding all four sides, cedar shakes that had been stained a gorgeous gray color from the sea, and enough room to fit ten people.

"I come here with my family when they visit," he explained when she noticed more children's drawings. "There isn't anything like this in Russia," he added, and they both laughed.

The house was two stories, with an open plan on the first floor. It was basically one massive room, meant for gathering and spending time together. The upstairs had many bedrooms and baths, each with magnificent views of the beach.

He brought her up to his bedroom almost as soon as they had arrived, and they made love while they listened to the sounds of the waves crashing. It was beautiful and romantic and she never wanted to go home.

She never asked him how long they were going to stay, because she dreaded the answer. She texted Daya and Asha, and her assistant, to let them know she was going away with Vlad for a little while. Other than that, she'd had no interaction with the outside world. There was no internet connection here and it felt rather freeing. She and Vlad had spent about ten days just really enjoying each other, and getting to know each other better. And of course, making love.

They went snorkeling, her very first foray into the world of breathing through a tube, and it was magical.

She could not believe the amount and variety of absolutely breathtaking fish there was to see! And they were everywhere. If she stuck her head underwater and opened her eyes, she didn't even have to move. They all just swam by, like her own tropical kaleidoscope.

But at some point, she knew this had to come to an end, and she and Vlad would have to head home. They had not discussed what would happen when they were back to their normal lives; she knew they were in a relationship, but it would be strange to not see him every day, and sleep with him every night.

I love him. So very, very much.

He quickly became the most important person in her world, but instead of feeling scared about that, she felt exhilarated. Simply because she knew that Vlad felt the same way about her. He was always so kind and sweet to her. He made sure she was comfortable and had everything she needed, before he worried about himself. It was the same in the bedroom, too. He was a very giving lover.

She pushed away the nagging thoughts of what would happen when he returned to Russia in two years. That was a long time from now, and a lot could happen between now and then. But as far as she was concerned, she wanted him in her life forever.

* * *

Vlad told her to be ready for dinner at eight o'clock.

But of course, he refused to tell her anything else.

Thania took a shower and slathered herself with lotion.

She did not wear any makeup while here, so she didn't

put any on. She simply slipped a long sarong around

her body and tied it between her breasts. With a pair of

bikini bottoms on, it was an outfit. In fact, it was

dressed up, she thought with a smile.

She walked down to the sea with Raphael as her guide. Raphael was Vlad's caretaker, and Vlad wanted her to meet him at a specific spot in order to watch the sunset together. So Raphael was making sure that she went the right way. She sighed. Vlad had done so many romantic things since they had arrived here; she would have to write them all down so she never forgot one single detail.

She said goodbye to Raphael and started to stroll toward the spot on the sand where they would have dinner. Vlad had already arranged a blanket and a basket of food, but he was nowhere to be seen. She walked up to the blanket and sat down. She had just popped the cork on some champagne, when she heard Vlad behind her.

"Don't turn around," his gravelly voice said in her ear, and she smiled.

Those were the first words he had ever spoken to her. His body as he knelt behind her felt just as delicious against her back now, as it had the day that they had met.

"I wish they had paired us together," he said, and she smiled wider.

Aww, he's being sentimental. I can't believe he's thinking the same thing right now.

"They should have known that we belong together," he continued softly against her ear. "Anyone within a mile of the two of us should be able to figure that out. I knew it the minute I saw you across that room, even though I was scared at the time. But I'm not scared anymore, Thania."

Her heart started to pound as she listened to him.

"I'm not scared, and I know what I want," he said as he came around and knelt in front of her. "I love you, Thania Walter. I am truly, madly, deeply in love with you, and I know that I will be for the rest of my life and beyond. I pray that you feel the same way about me."

She nodded at him because she was fighting back tears and couldn't speak.

"I don't care where we live. I don't care if I eventually must leave the jewelry company. I would follow you to the ends of the earth, in order to be with you."

"Vlad," she whispered, as tears fell down her cheeks.

"Shhh, I'm not done," he said, and she laughed.

"The next time you have a fashion show, I want to be front and center, watching with pride. I want someone to come up to me after the show, and I want to be able to tell them that I am Thania Walter's husband. I can think of nothing else that would make me more proud."

She smiled and cried at the same time, amazed at what he was saying to her. Then, he brought a tiny seashell from behind his back. It was one she had picked up on their many walks on the beach. It was perfect: inside was a rainbow of colors, all blended in to each other. When she'd found it, she'd told him, "this one reminds me of us," and he'd smiled and slipped it into his pocket.

As she looked down at it now, nestled at the bottom of the rainbow seashell, was a diamond ring. She brought her hands to her mouth and cried harder.

"Thania Walter," he said, "will you do me the honor of allowing me to become your husband? Would you stay with me, forever?"

"Yes! Oh my God, yes!" she managed, and they hugged and cried together.

Eventually, he slipped the ring on her finger, and she was speechless once again. It was a beautiful, huge, round diamond, surrounded in a circle by a single stone in every color of the rainbow.

* * *

They made love on the blanket, under the stars and next to the sea. They talked about how they both felt so incredibly blessed to have found one another. They talked about their future, and how many children they each hoped for: Thania wanted two and Vlad wanted seven. She laughed and told him to forget it.

They talked about her business and the success of the runway show. They talked about the jewelry company, and all that he had to do in the next coming years to achieve a good market share in America. They talked about their friends, and how odd it was that her two best girlfriends, and his two best guy friends, were all single. Maybe they would each find the happiness

that Vlad and Thania shared.

And then they laughed a little bit smugly, but they

could be forgiven—after all, they just received the

biggest gift that life had to offer—True Love.

Epilogue

Thania heard an annoying buzzing sound, and she tried to swat it away. It would not stop though, and it was right around her head, so she smacked the air.

"Ow!" Vlad said, and she looked over in the dark to see him rubbing his forehead.

"Sorry, love," she mumbled as she patted his naked behind. "Bug in here."

The sound was so loud and irritating now that Vlad had turned on the light in the bedroom in order to find it.

"Kill it!" she said, her face in her pillow. "Kill it right now, Vlad!"

The idea was not very charitable, Thania admitted to herself, but there you have it. They needed sleep, and it was the middle of the night. The bug must die. It really was that simple. Thania had come to terms with the arrangement.

Except the bug wasn't flying anywhere. And it wasn't a bug at all. The noise was coming from one spot, and Vlad hunted it down until he found it— Thania's hand bag.

"Do you want me to kill it?" he asked in a serious tone. "It's your phone," he said, tossing it lightly to her.

She sat up at the same time and the phone hit her on the nose. "Ow!" Thania said, wiping her watering eyes.

"Sorry, love," Vlad mumbled, as he got back into bed beside her and snuggled close.

She stared at her phone as if it was a foreign object. Which it sort of was, since she hadn't used it in going on two weeks now. But the damn thing would *not stop ringing*. There was some sort of international code on the screen so she didn't even know who it was that was calling her at this un-Godly hour.

"Hello!" she yelled into the phone after swiping the screen. She heard clicks and clangs and strange noises in the background, and she was just about to hang up when she heard her.

"Thania!" It was Asha, and she sounded hysterical, even through the poor international connection.

Thania sat straight up in bed.

"Asha! Asha!" she yelled into the phone, getting more and more distressed as the moments passed and she did not hear her friend's voice again.

Vlad got up out of bed and turned on the nightstand lamp. It was pitch black outside.

"Thania!" she heard again.

"Asha, what is it? What's wrong?" She knew beyond a shadow of a doubt that Asha would never contact her when she was away with Vlad, unless it was truly an emergency. Thania felt fear rush through her as she waited what seemed an interminably long time for Asha to speak again.

"I need you, Thania! I need you to come home!"

"Of course! We will come home immediately!" Thania was really in a panic now; she jumped out of bed and began gathering her things with one hand. Asha never asked anyone for anything.

"I need help, Thania!" Asha said, and Thania heard her crying.

Thania had never, in all of their years of being friends, ever seen Asha cry. She was momentarily stunned.

"What happened?" Thania yelled, trying to be heard over the clinks and clanks of the phone. Now the connection was so bad, that Asha's voice was coming in and out.

"He...me...need...can't...don't..."

It was all garbled, and she held the phone away from her ear and pressed speaker so that Vlad could listen also. Maybe if they both listened, they would be able to make out what she was saying. At that moment, the line became crystal clear, and Asha's crying voice

came through the phone as if she was standing in the
room with them.

"It's David!" she cried. "David's hurt me again."

* * *

Asha's story is told in Imani King's next novel, **Talk To Me**.

While Imani is writing her next book, would you like a sneak peek into her first Russian Billionaire novel? Shh, here it is…

Her Russian Billionaire, A BWWM Romance

Novel

An Excerpt

Chapter One

"Come on Michelle," I muttered to myself. "Get it together."

Leaning against the wall of the employee bathroom, I took what felt like my first breath in half an hour. I rubbed my freshly-scrubbed hands across my face, trying to pull myself together. I'd always been high-strung. But it was that very personality trait that had allowed me to graduate from medical school at the top of my class and procure a great internship at a very competitive hospital in Miami. At the moment, however, my nervous disposition seemed to be acting against me.

As an Emergency Medicine intern, I had very little experience with operating room procedures—at least not practical experience. Sure, I'd observed a number of surgeries during medical school and a few emergency surgeries in the ER since I'd been here. But I'd never seen anyone die on the operating table before today.

I had only been there to hold the retractors. Half of the surgical staff at Miami General had come down with a massive stomach virus, and I had been loaned out from the Emergency Room at the end of my night shift to act as another set of hands during a routine surgery. At the time, I'd jumped at the opportunity—when would I ever get to see a cardiac bypass surgery?

Thinking about that fact now, I cringed. I definitely did not need that experience at the cost of my nerves.

Hazarding a look in the mirror, I couldn't help but cringe again. My normally pretty face was ashen, and there were dark circles underneath my now-glassy golden brown eyes. My already kinky hair was frizzier than ever from spending the last few hours under a surgical cap. And, of course, there was blood all over my light blue scrubs. That was the final straw, and another wave of panic washed through my body.

Obviously, I had no problem with blood in and of itself—I would have no place in the medical field if I did. It was the memory of the death I'd just witnessed that had me trembling. I'd seen quite a few dead bodies over the years, but I'd never seen someone die right in front of me—while I was, at least partially, responsible for that person's wellbeing. I had always known that death was something I would need to get used to as an ER doctor, but this, as my very first experience, had been jarring.

I knew that I should at least change, if not shower, before heading home. Right now though, I was just trying to focus on standing without shaking, which didn't seem like a feat I could handle at the moment.

I heard the door of the bathroom open, and a cute girl with gorgeous seemingly pore-less caramel skin and short curly hair walked in. I recognized her as a resident in the surgery department, though I hadn't actually talked to her before. I was glad to see that I wasn't the only resident who weighed over one hundred and fifty pounds. It seemed that most doctors dealt with stress by not eating, while I was always known to turn to food to help me forget about the day's problems.

The girl smiled at me as she washed her hands. "You must be the emergency room intern who helped out with the triple bypass," she stated.

"Yeah," I answered, trying to keep my hand from trembling as I reached out to shake hers. "Michelle Carter."

"I'm Lori," she said with a smile. "Lori Hughes. I'm a surgical resident here."

"I know," I replied. "I've seen you around. It's nice to finally meet you."

"Yeah. Wish it were under better circumstances."

I cringed, realizing how fast news must have spread. I guess it was hard to miss the hustle and the alarms when someone stopped breathing on the operating table.

"Was that the first time you've seen someone die during an operation?" Lori asked when I didn't reply.

"Yeah," I whispered with a shaky breath, not trusting myself to say anything else.

Lori put a hand on my shoulder and squeezed gently. "Last year at about this time, I was in your same position. It gets easier. I mean, it still sucks, but it gets... less shocking, I guess."

"It was really unexpected."

"Yeah. It usually is. But from what I heard, he was old, and the triple-bypass was a little risky anyway."

I nodded, trying to focus on what she was saying.

"I would think you saw more death down in the ER than we see up here."

"I've been here less than a month," I explained with a shrug. "It hasn't happened yet during my shifts."

"Well," Lori said, squeezing my arm a little harder, "just remember that it wasn't your fault. There was nothing you could do. Go home and try to relax. It will get easier, I promise!"

"Thanks," I replied as Lori turned away. "It was good to meet you."

"You too," Lori said over her shoulder, with the most genuine smile I'd seen since I'd moved here. "I'm sure I'll see you around."

After Lori left, I took another minute to collect myself before heading downstairs to shower and change in the ER locker room.

I had completed an entire shift in the ER before volunteering to help out on the surgery, so I was physically and mentally exhausted by the time I finally dragged myself through the door of my tiny apartment.

Curling up on the sofa, I wrapped in one of my grandmother's quilts, with a bowl of ice cream serving as dinner (even though it was technically breakfast time) and a glass of wine on the coffee table in front of me. The doctor inside me cringed at the nutritional content of my food, but I really couldn't garner the strength to feel too guilty about my choices for sustenance right now.

Unfortunately, food had become a coping
mechanism for me in the recent months. During my
final year at med school in Chicago, my boyfriend
dumped me because he believed that I wasn't
"committed enough" to our relationship. I had
completely rearranged by life to suit him, but I hadn't
been willing to sacrifice my grades, which is what, in
the end, Scott had deemed a "lack of commitment."
Plus, as he never ceased to emphasize, he felt like I
wasn't "committed to staying fit, healthy, and
attractive." He had maliciously pointed out that I'd
gained some extra weight since we'd started dating.
Yes, I'd gained some weight... but I spent all of my free

time with him – had even sacrificed sleep to keep our relationship strong. Between school and Scott, I hadn't had time to exercise or worry about what I ate.

The positive side of Scott dumping me was that I had even more time to focus on school. I was already near the top of my class, but with more time to study I quickly rose to number one. This allowed me the pick of many desirable internship positions. And, without Scott, I also had the freedom to choose a residency program anywhere in the country, not having to worry about staying close to my boyfriend. Plus, my mom hated that I was dating a white guy anyway. But she hated everyone I've ever dated. That was one of the reasons why I ended up in Miami. I'd been here once, on a spring break of my junior year at college, and I just fell in love with the culture and energy of the people here. Getting away from my super-controlling mom was a definite bonus.

It seemed like a great change at the time, but now I found myself so far away from everyone I knew and loved, truly alone for the first time in my life. I hadn't quite clicked with the rest of my cohort of interns, and today's shock had shaken my confidence in the one thing I was still sure of—my ability to be a good doctor.

"I'm not going to cry," I told myself aloud, willing that statement to be true. Instead of giving in to tears, I took a large, rich bite of Rocky Road, savoring the taste

of chocolate and marshmallows and washing it down

with a sip of Malbec. Once I was finished with the ice

cream, I set the bowl on the table and I wrapped myself

fully in the quilt. Finally, I allowed the tears to flow

freely down my face, promising myself that tomorrow

would be another day.

Chapter Two

Unfortunately, by the time my shift began the following morning, news of the surgical mishap had traveled down to the Emergency Room. It felt like the other two of the other ER interns, Kyle Martin and Julia Gimbal, took turns snickering about it over the course of the day. I tried to remind myself that they were probably jealous that I'd been chosen to help out in the surgery and were treating me accordingly.

"Look on the bright side," Julia said at one point with a fake smile, "you'll probably never have to help out in surgery again."

We both knew that Julia would've killed for the opportunity to help in surgery, knowing how ambitious she was, but I chose not to point out that fact. Instead, I took comfort from the knowledge that she was obviously threatened by me.

"We both know I had nothing to do with what happened," I replied with a smile, channeling confidence I didn't actually feel. "In fact, Dr. Taylor commended me on my performance."

With that, I turned and walked away, pretending like Julia and Kyle's attitudes didn't bother me. I watched them later, chatting casually with each other, and couldn't help the pang of loneliness I felt.

This has nothing to do with me personally, I kept repeating to myself. It's not that I wanted to be included in their snarky little group, but having a friend would be nice. I couldn't help but wish that Lori had been a member of my intern group—how different things could have turned out if she had been. I made a mental note to ask her out for coffee soon.

Things were getting back to normal by the end of the week—as normal as they could be in any

Emergency Room, that is. The gossip had died down and, though I still wasn't getting along great with the other interns, they were no longer being outright snarky to me.

I'd also begun to accept the death I'd witnessed in the operating room as a learning experience—just part of the job. Theoretically, I had always known that patients sometimes died during surgeries, but now that knowledge was a little more first-hand. I decided to stop thinking about it and move on.

That all changed, however, when I was called into the Department Chair's office on Friday afternoon.

"Michelle, welcome," Dr. Viola Grimes said as she ushered me into her office and motioned for me to sit.

Dr. Grimes was in her mid-forties, with short greying hair and wire-rimmed glasses. She had always been nice to me, yet I couldn't help but find her intimidating. As the only African American female physician on staff of the Emergency Room, she kind of took me under her wing from the start. She'd been at Miami General for decades and was one of the most respected doctors in the hospital—and in the field. Being able to work under her guidance was one of the other reason I chose this hospital for my internship. Hesitantly, I took a seat across from her.

"So, Michelle, why don't you tell me about your experience helping out in surgery the other day," Dr. Grimes said once I was comfortable.

I opened my mouth, but nothing came out. I wasn't sure what to say. Surely, I wasn't in trouble, right?

"I… I was there just to help. There isn't much I can tell you, the other doctors would probably have more details. I was just holding the retractors. Then, when the patient began to crash, I switched positions with another attending, who helped attempt to get the situation under control."

"That's what it says in the file here," Dr. Grimes pushed the folder across her desk towards me.

I wasn't sure what to do, so I remained quiet.

"The reason I've asked you here," Dr. Grimes continued, "is because this case has been chosen for presentation at the next month's Morbidity and Mortality conference. Are you familiar with what that is?"

"Yes," I replied, relieved to finally discuss something I was comfortable with. "An M&M conference is a regular review of complications and errors made during the patient's hospital stay. Cases are reviewed, system errors are identified, and ways of improving patient care are discussed."

"Well," Dr. Grimes said with a smile, "you sure have the textbook definition down. But that's basically it." She paused. "And you have been chosen to present this case at the next month's conference."

"What?" I sat forward, confused. "Surely, there are people with far more experience than I have that could present the case."

"Yes," Dr. Grimes replied with a knowing smile. "Unfortunately, none of them want the added chore. This is the kind of thing that often gets pushed off to the lowest person on the totem pole. And for this particular case, that person is you."

Dr. Grimes motioned for me to take the file sitting in front of me on her desk. Tentatively, I picked it up.

"Don't look so mortified," she said with a chuckle. "It really isn't that bad. No one is going to blame you for anything that happened. You are just there to present the facts and answer the questions. M&M presentation experience is great for any intern. It's a good skill to have."

I perked up a little at that. I always leapt at the chance to learn new things. Which, I reminded myself, is what got me into this in the first place.

"Okay," I said, nodding, finally able to offer her a real smile. "I can do this!"

"Sure you can. All you need to do is familiarize yourself with the details of the case and be prepared to answer questions. There may be a little more scrutiny than normal for this case in particular, as the man who died, Charles McDaniel, was our senator's brother-in-law. We want to make sure all of our bases are covered in the event of any litigation."

My eyebrows went up at the word *litigation*, but I didn't want to ask. Instead I just nodded some more. Dr. Grimes rose and slowly walked towards the door, signifying the end of our meeting.

"If you need help or have questions," Dr. Grimes said as I exited her office, "there are a few residents who have presented cases in the past and can give you pointers. I'm sure you can find someone willing to help."

Nodding, I made my way back to the Emergency Room.

"What was that about?" Julia asked, obviously alerted to my meeting with Dr. Grimes. I couldn't help but wonder how her and Kyle were always so well informed. "Did you get in trouble?"

"No," I replied with a smile, trying not to let her see how nervous I was. "I was asked to present the case of that operating room fatality at the next month's M&M conference."

I could see the jealousy in Julia's eyes, so I turned and left before she could start badgering me about it. Instead, I headed up to surgery to see if I could find Lori again.

As luck would have it, Lori was in the surgeons' lounge, reviewing a file with a few other people.

"Michelle, right?" she asked with a smile when she noticed me. I nodded. "How are you doing?"

"Much better," I replied with a smile of my own. "I was wondering… and it's okay if you don't have time to help, but… have you ever had to present a case at an M&M conference?"

"Oh yeah," Lori replied with a laugh. "We all have." Lori motioned to the other two people sitting with her. They nodded in agreement. "Those are usually pushed off on an intern or resident. None of the doctors ever want to do them."

"Glad I'm not alone," I said. "I really don't know where to start. Is there any way I could pick your brain at some point?"

"Sure," Lori replied, looking at her watch. "My shift is about to end and I'll have a few minutes before I have to get home to relieve my babysitter. Have a seat."

Feeling much more encouraged than I had been only moments earlier, I sat down next to Lori and her friends and began reviewing the case.

End of excerpt

To continue reading Her Russian Billionaire, go to this link:

http://www.amazon.com/dp/B0122901ZA

About the Author

Imani King is a small town girl with a big imagination. She nurtures a passion for yoga and can often be found in the studio when she's not writing. In her fantasies, she and her billionaire Mr. Right travel the world, exploring different cultures and each other! These daydreams are the inspiration for her sizzling stories, so what are you waiting for? Give one of them a try and let her know what you think.

Author Central: www.amazon.com/author/

imaniking

Facebook: https://www.facebook.com/pages/

Imani-King/576103915864425

Newsletter: http://eepurl.com/blwtg5

Made in the USA
Lexington, KY
16 January 2017